NIGHTMARE
IN
ELM CITY

MaineyO

"Nightmare in the Elm City"
- MaineyO.
"King & Queen Publishing."
Copyright © 2021
ISBN:

Cashapp: $kingqueenpublishing

Instagram Page: @king.queenpublishing

Facebook Page: @kingandqueenpublishing

Website: https://www.kingandqueenpublishing.org/

Email: info@kingandqueenpublishing.org

Dedication

This book is dedicated to my children; Donqwa, Dejanae, Devontae, and Damani Ogman.

I am also dedicating this book to my grandparents; Tillman and Sarah Mcfadden, rest their souls.

My father, Big Don, Rest in Peace.

Finally, I dedicate this book to King and Queen Publishing.

Thank you for giving me this opportunity to show off my writing skills.

Acknowledgment

My sisters, Makia and Lanisha Richardson. My brothers, Gary and Messy. I love you all to death there are no words to express how I feel. Saying the word, 'love you all to death' is not enough. It's way more than that. Mom, you are the strongest woman in the world. I'm sorry for all the pain I put you through, if I gotta lay my life down for you to have the world, I'm not going to think twice about that, I love you Dollbaby Julie McFadden. To my neices and nephews, I love you all; from Uncle Maine. Kejaun you better make it to the NBA don't let that talent go to waste.

This is for all the real ones that are locked up and going through the struggle. I know the feeling, trust me, it's real! But keep your head up and continue to fight this corrupt disparity system. Free a segal street general, the great one lizard nate, love u boy! Keep fighting never give up, we will meet again. Free Olie, G-bo, Huey, Mike Pun, Dipper, FattyM, Hillbill, BabyR, Dev, Pun, Moe Dizo keep fighting, you clearly shown them at trial you was innocent, but somehow they still found you guilty with no evidence backing they played. Keep fighting, love u bro!

Nasty from the Bx lil bro free him. Tythrone free him, Budda from the 2.5. free him, Tank, Blu, and Pooh Bear my jersey Bros free them. My lil cuz Terelle Free him, My guy C-

note from Chi-town Free him, Brown Eyes from the beat free
him, N'sane from Louisville keep fightin big cuz, to get that life
sentence off of u, keep faith!

All my real niggaz In United State Penitentiary Canaan Free
them! Shout out to JoJo, Cousin Patty, Jr, Budda, Kev green
Eyes, City, Brock, Dev, Rb, marv, D-man, Core, Dice aka Sniper,
Dodo, Slay, Gotti, Dayday, Leek, S.t., CoCo, Skillet, Boone, Big
Bub aka Big Worm, Killa Can, Aunty Shirley, C.R, Plizzy,
Twistdownz, Hussle, Greg "A" Donna, Uncle Joe Boyd, Duke,
and Natalie plus the whole Boyd Family, Killa Jay, Nitty Redd,
Big Ether stay in the studio you fire Scav, you're going to blow!

Sade Ragland, Amy Kent my favorite white Girl, Bucc
The Scav, Pusher, Sherelle love u lil sis, you a real one. Animal
Cub, my lil nigga held it down, you a real one! Klept what up my
guy, Pizzy.

Thanks for holding my sis down, Ratchet, Bless, D.p.p legend
Mary sola, N.O, My cousin Jones love u bro, Kina, Net and
Nelly what up. Terena, Lingo, Amber, Bj, Daisey, Lil Quasha,
thank u for your Love , Michelle Britt, My D.C guy Shooes, free
him also.

Gina Gine love you cuz, Deneda and Hon love you all.
Kita and Dayona what up. Holly Lexy, Cruger, Cherokee, love u

ma. Jason hall, Twan Blacc, Sheila Washington and the whole Washington, Greens, and Hall family. Aunt Tina aka Dirt, love you lady. Tripple Black what up cuz, Shiriz what up my guy.

Tasha Soloman, Bianca, MaineBall, Binky Aka bink ladin, my Fair Haven guys, Norm, Mike Mas, BuckyB, Quisy, Bigs and Willy. Bear Back, DayDay Miller, Tee the Scav, Cheree Bailey, Nue stay beautiful baby, always will love u, Tae, Lil Ug, Quicey, Teeida, Glenn, Lil cuz Lex.

My second mother Aunty Cookie, Mel Black, Bubii. Shout out to the whole Mcfadden, Moore, and Baker Family, Diamond Davis, Chello, Thuggish, Shana aka SBlocc, Shamar aka Lil Marky-D, love you boy! Sharonda "RonRon" Boston, shout out to the whole Boston Family, Shanae Ham, Moochy, Hot Nik, Logic, G-Early, 9 fingers nitty.

To my whole Indictment, the ones that did what men suppose to do, and shut the fuck up, you're all real ones. The pressure was real even as a female, Jan had shut the fuck up when it was real, love u Jan. Aunty Peaches and Rose thank so much for being there for me love you all more. Travis, what up bro, Lil sis Diamond Robinson love u sis, Uncle Ghost, Champ, Aj, and Boogie what up love you all...Lil cuz Jaday, thank u for always checking up on big cuz, love you more for that.

My GrandMother HoneyMa, love you. Shout out to the whole Ogman family. GIP MarkyD, the town was crushed when u left us. Love you Cro, Dada, Pj, Tymac. RIP Coov, JesWes, Pelly pel, My lil Bro North Up Hovito, Smurf, Billy Ray, Douggie, Quay, Foot, Tommie Gunz, Quintel, Cousin Fred and Mel, D-Lover, Kurt SkeeeeediBe, Buck Marley, Carmelo, Typer, Mel Oscar, Stevens street legends Uncle Hop, Mike Bev, T-Rock, Dre, Mone Lush, Shelton, Big Disco, Johnny Gore, and freak....Rip Kiana Jenkins, Desiree Amin, Smurf, Diamond Shelby Shel, you a Hill legend, Cousin Tray, Knoot.

My aunty Thelma, Uncle Sonny, Willy, Richard, Aunty Carol, Gloribel, My cuz freaky-Ty miss u cuz rest up.

Micheal BooBoo Edwards, I'm still hurting from this one, you really fuck me up, Day one, always my Bro. Almost two year, and I'm still crushed, love u Bro rest up.

Uncle Duke, Benji and Joe Black miss you all and love you all...The Hill is my Home.

Shout out to the Tre, West Hills J-Hood, what up, Island, Ville, Tribe, Fair Haven, West haven, Hamden, Ansonia, Rockview, and out the way...Franklin Street aka The Ghetto, Better Known as the "G" Wat up.

The whole Elm city..Segal St. what up, Congress Ave, Ann and Kussuth St., Congress and West, Davenport Ave, Elliot St., WE THE NORTH SANCTION...Shout out to the whole Hill 06519 sanction....To the Scavies, I thank you all very much for the support you have been showing over the years, you shown what a brotherhood is about and we also show we could walk down a positive path, we built this and I love you all for it, thank you! Lil full force what up heart 2 heart.

Last but not the least, Pre, you are one of my most favorite in the world. You are a definition of what real is about. Thank you for not judging me all these years, you have been the same and always uplifted me when people I love, cross me or turn their back on me, you are always there; love u! Stay a baddie and I'm giving you your flowers now, you sanction!!! Thanks for the ones that was there for me during the time when it was real, thank you for hearing me out and pressing #5 to hear me vent out from all the stress. Thank you and I appreciate all the love and support. I am also grateful to the ones that sent letters to my judge you all rock that!!! Still pending in court....

Elm City and urban readers everywhere, enjoy the Book, part 2 is going to be even better.

Elm city series presents, NIGHTMARE IN ELM CITY.

Prologue

Nashawn and Demi hopped on the City bus on Congress Ave, on their way to play ball at the open gym at Webster. Every neighborhood in New Haven had an open gym or some kind of after-school program for the youth, to help them stay out of trouble. Webster is a school in the Tribe neighborhood. Nashawn always wanted to display his sick-basketball talent and Webster's open gym was the talk of the town. All the best players wanted to play ball there, but what Nashawn and Demi G didn't understand was why only certain hoods were allowed to play.

"Ayo cuz, you always want to go and show off. Got us going all the way to the Tribe, I hate going to other projects since the last time I got jumped in the G, but I get it tho...I'm with you." Said Demi G.

"Shit, it's fun as hell dunking on these niggas, plus I heard there are mad chicks there. Your little girlfriend crush is going to be there anyway.... Little pretty Nue.... Ha, ha, ha." Nashawn said, while laughing at his right-hand man.

"Man shut up with that Nue shit." Said Demi.

"Nigga, you ain't got to lie to me! That's the only real reason why you going .... To see Nue!" said Nashawn.

They got off the B-bus and boarded the D-bus going to Dixwell Ave.

"I got something to tell you, Demi." Said Nashawn.

"What you got to tell me?" Demi asked.

"I got down with Stevens Street Posse." Said Nashawn.

All throughout the 80's Stevens street was known for being a million-dollar block and also known for its violence.

"Damn. You really got down with S.S.P.?" Asked Demi.

"Hell yeah! They got all the power, especially Dre, Mone Lush, and Disco. I look up to them niggas."

They approached Webster's on Dixwell Ave, both Nashawn, and Demi G were nervous, walking by the Tribe projects to get to Webster's. They entered the community center; it had about 200 kids all over Webster. There were about 100 in the big gym, and they all was from the Tribe. Demi and Nashawn headed towards the bleachers. Nashawn took his shorts and kicks out of his book-bag and called Next, Demi just looked around, while he sat next to Nashawn until he saw Nue.

Nue walked over to them both from a crowd of Tribe chicks.

"I told you not to come here", said Nue

" I know, but you never told me why?" Said Demi

"Because Demi, it's Tribe only here." Said Nue.

On the other side of the gym there were two heavyset 12-year-olds, the same age as Nashawn and Demi. Shana walked over to them and asked, "where y'all from?''

Demi got his ass whooped in the G a couple years back for this same shit, but in the Elm, if you ain't claiming your hood, you are considered a bitch!

"The Hill.'' Demi and Nashawn said at the same time to Shana. Shana turned around to where Pizzy and Bout It were at, and yelled to them, *"The Hill!!!''*

The whole gym got quiet. *"See, I told you Demi; you shouldn't have come here!"*

Demi and Nashawn just sat there as they watched two big ass-niggas walk towards them.

"Damn! We bout to get our ass whooped! Fucking with you, Nashawn!" said Demi.

"I don't give a fuck! Fuck these Tribe niggas, it's whatever.'' Said Nashawn.

"Hold the fuck up! Where y'all from?'' Asked Pizzy.

"Nigga! I said I'm from the fucking Hi.....CRACCK!"

Pizzy punched Nashawn in the mouth before he could finish saying the word Hill. CRACKKK! Bout It hooked off on Demi. Both of them were trying to make run for it, but there were too

11

many of them everywhere. Demi and Nashawn were swinging-straight haymakers. Demi managed to get free and left through the emergency exit, but realized Nashawn wasn't by his side. So Demi ran back to get his best friend and saw about 20 Tribe-niggas taking turns, punching and kicking his best friend. Demi looked around trying to find a weapon, he saw a fire extinguisher and grabbed it off the wall. Demi ran into the gym and started spraying it on all the faces of them Tribe-niggas.

"Nigga, come on!" Demi yelled to Nashawn. Nashawn's eyes was fucked up bad, he could barely see. Demi grabbed his arm.

"Come on Nashawn." Said Demi, as the Tribe-niggas struggled to see through the cloud of white smoke from the fire extinguisher.

"Run nigga!" Said Demi. They both ran out of the gym. Nue led them to another exit door, so as to go outside before they ran into more Tribe niggas. They were running their fastest through the Tribe.

"Oh shit! We can't even get on the bus. I left my book-bag with all my stuff in it." Said Nashawn.

"Fuck that book-bag! We all fucked up, we might as well walk home." Said Demi. And that's what they did. Once they got to Stevens street in the Hill, they were happy.

"I knew we shouldn't have went there Nigga." Said Demi.

"You wanted to see Nue, so, stop fronting." Said Nashawn.

"Yeah and I got my ass whooped right in front of her." Said Demi.

"Fuck it! We got our ass whooped!" They both started laughing.

"I love you, bro", said Demi.

"I love you too, bro!" Nashawn said.

"We are best friends for life! We ain't never going to let nothing get between us bro!" Said Demi.

"Pinky swears!"

Demi and Nashawn locked pinkes, and both said, *"Best friends forever…. For life."*

"O yeah, another thing." Said Nashawn.

"What?" Asked Demi.

"We going to keep tonight a secret between us!" Said Nashawn. They both started laughing, thinking about how they had to run from getting beaten to death.

"Okay, brothers for life. Our secret." Said Demi.

13

"Brothers to the end!" Said Nashawn. They embraced one another with a hug.

In the Elm City, no one can be trusted. Not even your own flesh and blood brother. New Haven earned the name "Pistol Waving" for a reason. Live by it, or die by it! "Where you from?" is the everyday saying in New Haven and whatever hood you from is your identity.

As a result, here in New Haven, we claim our hoods respectfully and with pride, because it's who we are....... Safety first, is what the whole Elm City says to each other because it might be the last time you see each other. Nashawn and Demi made a bond, or did they? Brothers forever right? Well, I will let y'all be the judge of that. Rep your hood, where are you from.

Chapter One

- Fall of 2002 -

Ding Dong! Ding Dong!

"Demi! Get the door. You know it ain't nobody but that nappy-headed boy for you," Ms. Edwards yelled from the bathroom, as she was getting dressed for work.

"C'mon mom. Why you always gotta talk about Greatness?"

"Great what? What is that boy great at besides getting into troubles?"

"Basketball."

"Well...." Ms. Edwards was at loss for words for a few moments because despite all Greatness' shortcomings, no one could deny that he was something special on that court. Standing at around 6'1 with unlimited range and crazy hops, he was most definitely a NBA prospect. He's had the attention of many divisions from college coaches since the 8th grade. Now, if only he could stay out of his own way.

"If he doesn't become smart, he won't be playing in nobody's NBA. He's gonna be dead or in jail."

Demi didn't respond. He's heard all this from his mother before. He was saved from hearing it again by the ring of the doorbell.

"Well, saved by the bell."

"Bye mom, love you."

Demi laughed as he ran out of the room, leaving Ms. Edwards shaking her head.

"Damn Nigga, it took your ass long enough" Greatness said, giving Demi some Dap.

"Shit, it takes time to look this good. I know you didn't think I woke up looking like this."

"Man, whatever." Greatness said, laughing, as he checked out Demi's outfit. Both of them were fly as usual. Demi we wearing a pair of blue Polo jeans, a striped polo button-down, with matching Jordans. Greatness had on a red white, and blue Fila track-suit, with the matching Fila sneaks and hat.

"Come on, I parked the car over on Congress Ave," Greatness said, as he started walking up the block. The blocks in the Hill used to be something straight off of a Hallmark card. Big, beautiful green Elm trees lined the majority of New Haven's streets which gave New Haven the nickname, "The Elm City". Strictly because of the tall, lush trees. By the mid 90's, the nickname symbolized something else..... Money. The green represented all the money that came through the city, the root of all evil.

"Whose shit is this?" Demi asked, as he hopped into the passenger side of a 88 Delta.

"This old head named Clyde from the Ville." Greatness responded.

"Oh yeah, I know Old Head. How did you get his car?"

"Man, all I had to do was give him four of those big-ass dimes my cousin Tae is selling."

"Bro, Tae gonna fuck you up if you keep stealing his shit!" Demi said, laughing. Greatness shot back as he pulled away from the curb. The ride to James Hill-house High school across town didn't take long.

They got there about 15 minutes early, giving them enough time to stunt for all the little cuties. All of them breaking necks to speak, *"hey Greatness, I like your car. Ooh my God, Demi, your sneakers are so cute."*

"Y'all better strap Wilbur cross' ass on Friday. We're all coming to the game." This went on for about 10 minutes or so before Demi suddenly hopped out of the car truck, and started walking towards the school.

"Damn Nigga! You're whipped. You don't move that fast when we're on a fast break." Greatness yelled at Demi's back.

"Fuck you!" Demi shouted back, never breaking his stride as he continued toward his girl, Mary, who was walking up the block.

"Hey Bae," Mary said, as she hugged Demi. Her smile, lighting up her face.

"I thought you were gonna call me back last night?" Mary said, as she folded her arms across her chest and pouted.

"I did call you back Bro, like 4 times. Your line was busy."

"Oh.... I must have knocked it off the hook when I fell asleep."

"Uh hum ..... Now, you owe me for accusing me of not calling you back."

Mary smiled. *"What do you want?"*

"*You*", Demi said, pulling her body close against his.

"You already got me silly." Mary said, smiling.

"You know what I mean," Demi said, as he slid his hands down her body until they met her butt.

"Demi stop, nasty." Mary said, blushing hard as she pulled away. *"Everybody is looking at us."*

"So what! Let 'em look. You're mine. All of this is mine," Demi said, while palming her butt, pulling her up against his hardness.

"Um .... Demi ...." Mary finally managed to pull-free.

"C'mon Bae. We are gonna be late." Mary grabbed his hand and pulled him towards the school building. Demi followed along, but clearly not happy about the situation. Once they made it to Mary's class, she hugged him and kissed him goodbye. *"Baby, just be patient a little bit longer, okay? I'm gonna make it up to you."*

"Shit .... you better. Get me running around here with blue balls and shit." Mary laughed as she walked into the classroom. *"Call me later today."*

"I will." Demi responded, before heading to his first period class.

The rest of the school day was uneventful. Demi met Greatness outside the building, then the two walked around the corner to the car.

"Bro, what time you going to the block?" Greatness asked, *"I don't know. Why what's up?"*

"Some niggas from Rock-view were talking about betting some bread."

"Doing what? I know they ain't talking about playing ball."

"Hell yeah! They're gonna meet us at the park. (Roberto Clemente Park)"

"Shit, you know I'm with it. That's free money."

"You already know ..... So what's up with you and Mary?" Greatness asked as he pulled off.

"We cool."

"Y'all cool?"

"Yeah we cool. We chilling."

"Y'all chilling? Hold the fuck up! Man, you still ain't hit that yet?"

Demi hesitated a moment too long. *"Dawg, she still ain't give you no pussy?"*

"She wanted to wait a while." said Demi.

"Wait a while? For what?" Greatness burst out laughing.

"What the hell you laughing for?"

"Dawg, I know you don't think that Mary still a virgin?" Demi hesitated again. Greatness started laughing even harder. *"Man, what the fuck so funny?"* Demi yelled, starting to really get frustrated.

Greatness could see that Demi was getting mad, so he eased up a little.

"Nothing Dawg, I was just messing with you."

"Nah Bro, tell me."

Greatness looked at Demi, deciding whether he should hurt his little feelings or not. You'd be surprised how many dudes would rather stay in the dark when it comes to those hoes. *"Man, it ain't that serious. All I'm saying is that Mary ain't no virgin."*

Demi didn't say anything, he just stared at Greatness. *"My G, she's been fucking since like 5th and 6th grade. You remember light-skin Cee?"*

Demi shook his head yeah. Cee was a dude from the Southside part of the Hill, a few years older than them.

"He was fucking Mary back then; he was fucking her for like a whole summer."

Now that Demi really thought about it, he knew it was true. He could remember like three years ago, Cee used to always give them rides homes; he would always drop Mary off last. Even in the 6th grade, Mary's body was over-developed for a twelve-year-old. By the time she turned thirteen, her breasts were already D-cups. Her thighs and ass were thicker than all the other girls her age, and she was already getting her period.

21

"And don't forget about Slay," seeing the confusion on Demi's face, Greatness was hesitant before continuing, *"Demi, don't trip, I'm not saying she's a whore or anything like that. Mary's my girl, she's a cool person. I'm just saying she's not a virgin ..... Shit! She probably waiting on you. You know your game is weak as fuck."*

"Nigga, whatever." Demi smiled, thankful for Greatness not making shit worse.

"I bet you'll hit that shit this weekend."

"Now, that's what I'm talking about."

"Looks like one victim is here." Greatness said, as he pulled up to park, and saw the Kid, El and his boys.

"Well, let's go get this free money. We win a few games; you can take Mary out somewhere beside McDonald's .... Then, maybe she'll give your broke ass some pussy."

"Yeah, let's handle business, this shit shouldn't take long...."

- - -

"I told y'all this bum can't check me!"

"Man, clear out, clear the hole. This shit is over." Everyone cleared out, leaving Greatness and his man one-on-one.

Greatness smiled, as he looked in the face of the guy guarding him. The Kid was shocked; he could see it in his face.

Greatness dribbled the ball; left to right, right to left, back and forth through his legs as he moved slowly towards Jay. Jay got low in a defensive stance, Greatness noticed he opened his legs a little too-wide, now he knew he had him. Greatness threw the basketball right through Jay's legs. Jay was spinning around, but Greatness had already snatched the ball back as he stepped-sprinted to his right, Jay turned to go with him. Then Greatness quickly switched directions with a vicious crossover. Jay tried to adjust to Demi's sudden change of directions, his feet got tangled up and he went down.

"Ohhhhh!!!"

"Damnn!!!"

Everybody went crazy. Greatness finished off the play with a thunderous windmill dunk. The crowd went bananas. Dudes running on the court, yelling.

"Game time.... Give me my money, nigga." Greatness *shouted, as he high-fived his team.*

"Nigga, fuck you." Jay said, as he and his boys packed up their stuff. *"Son, don't get mad, y'all niggas know y'all couldn't fuck with us."* Demi joked, as Jay and his crew walked towards their jeep.

23

"Ayo, what the fuck you doing, Jay?" Greatness asked, as he followed them to their jump.

"Nigga, what does it look like? I'm leaving." Jay said, as he turned around to face Greatness.

"Yeah right, he better get my bread right first."

"Fuck you, nigga." Jay started, getting loud. *"I'm not giving you ...."* That's all he got out before Greatness took off on him. Demi, who wasn't far behind Greatness, followed up with a hook of his own and Jay went down once again. They were stomping his ass out by the time his homies made it back out the jeep. They jumped into the fight and it was a big free-for-all.

This only went on for about 2 minutes before.

Blocka! Blocka! Blocka!

"Oh shit!"

Everybody stopped fighting once they heard the gun shots, a few people even dove and hit the deck.

"Man, don't make me pop one of you niggas!"

Everybody looked at Black, who was standing there holding a black 9mm pistol. Black was a young wild Nigga from the Tre. His name was buzzing on the street, rumor has it he had already caught two bodies, or at least two that people knew about.

"Jay, Tone, y'all niggas come on, get in the jeep."

As they backed away towards the jeep, Greatness made a move to get at Jay.

"C'mon dawg, just let it go. This shit is not that serious." Demi said, holding Greatness back.

"Fuck you man, it ain't that serious?" Greatness spat, snatching his arm away before turning to face Demi.

"Like I said .... It's not that serious." Demi said, not backing down.

"It's only $500 my nigga." Demi continued.

"Fuck that money, Dawg; those bitch-ass niggas tried to clown us. Then that nigga, 'Black' is gonna grip up on us! Now, my nigga; we can't let that go at least I know I can't."

Greatness stared at Jay and Black as they drove off before saying his goodbye to Stretch, and they then headed towards the Delta.

Once inside, he immediately put a tape in and turned the music all the way up, letting Demi know that he wasn't in the mood to talk. Demi took the hint and they were both left there in their thoughts, as Styles P played through the speaker.

Chapter Two

"Oh my GOD ....Fuck!" Sade cried out, as Joey Ghost continued to pound her tight, wet pussy from the back.

"Now, don't run now, bitch." Ghost growled as he gripped Sade's hips, driving deeper and deeper.

"Ummm...Fu..ck...you...nig...ga." Sade was trying her best to talk shit back, but she knew she was fighting a losing battle. She was about to say something else when Ghost flipped her on to her back then started stroking her pussy from the front.

"Aaargghhh!" Sade cried out in pain and ecstasy as Ghost pounded more . He put her legs over his shoulders, pulling her to the edge of the mattress until her plump ass was hanging off and went to work. Ghost secured Sade with a vice-grip, so she couldn't do nothing but take the punishment.

"Uh huh."

"What old nigga you know can fuck like this?"

Sade's only response was moans and groans as Ghost beat up her tight walls. The sight of Sade's titties bouncing, and her eyes rolling in the back of her head was driving Ghost into a frenzy.

"Oh fuck .... Kill .... Umph, Umph ...this ...... mmphh, Mmphh ... pussy !!!" Ghost did his best to hold back, trying to spilt her little ass into two. He knew she was getting close to

26

cumming, because he could feel her pussy gripping and squeezing his manhood tighter so he began to massage her clit swiftly as he thrust deeply. After about 15 seconds, her body started to convulse and she screamed out as she creamed all over his swollen pole.

"Oh fuck! Aaaarrrgggghhhhh!" Ghost slammed his dick in her about three or four more times before her tight, greasy pussy became too much to handle. Ghost came hard, emptying his kids inside of her before collapsing on top of her.

"Happy Birthday old man." Sade teased as she massaged his head, neck, and back.

Ghost chuckled before kissing her on the lips. At 35 years old, Ghost was far from an old man, but when Ghost and Sade first met, she was 18 years old, and he joked with her saying, *"they didn't have any time to waste"* being that most niggas from the hood didn't live to see 50 years old, and he was already middle age. So, Ghost made sure they were going to live their lives to the fullest.

He had just taken one of Sade's nipples into his mouth, ready for round 2 when the doorbell rang.

"Shit!"

"Boy, stop faking. You know you need a few minutes to get ready for this pussy again."

Ghost dick was already rock-hard again, dripping his manhood, he began teasing Sade.

Rubbing the head of his swollen dick back and forth between Sade's wet ass pussy lips and fat clit.

"Ummmm boy...... you better stop." Sade cried out, as Ghost began slapping his dick against her throbbing pussy.

"Aawww Gooddd."

Sade's body convulsed as she exploded, her juices soaking the sheets.

"Ummm.... What the fuck did you just do to me?" Ghost just looked at Sade as she came down from her orgasmic high and smirked, getting dressed.

"Well, I guess you can teach an old dog new tricks, huh?" Ghost mumbled, as he grabbed himself; before walking out the room leaving Sade stuck and speechless.

"Damn old head, took you long enough." Demi said, as Ghost opened the door.

"What's up little bro?" Ghost asked, as he let in Demi G.

"I almost thought you weren't here." Demi said, sitting down on the couch.

"I was in the middle of something. What's up though?"

28

Demi was about to respond when Sade, descending down the stairs caught his attention.

"Damn!" was all Demi could say as Sade walked in.

Ghost smiled, as he caught Demi's eyes, *"Like I said, I was in the middle of something."*

"Hey handsome." Sade greeted Demi, before bending to give him a hug.

"What's up, Sade?" Demi mumbled, blushing as he felt her hard nipples pressing against him.

"Nothing much, about to make lunch. You hungry?"

"You know that little nigga is hungry. All he does is eat." Ghost responded for Demi, and that made Sade laugh.

"Alright, give me like 15 minutes, I got y'all." Sade said, before switching her fine ass to the kitchen. Demi watched her fat ass jiggle beneath her thin, tight, silk robe. Sade was the spitting image of a young Nia Long. She just had a little bit more weight in her ass, hips and thighs.

"You better find something more your speed. That one there will turn your young ass out." Said Ghost, laughing ......

"What chu talking about, old head?" Demi asked, as he finally tore his eyes away from that mesmerizing sight.

"Yeah aight. You know what I'm talking about little nigga. Anyway, what's up with you? Why you not on the block?"

"Greatness....." Demi responded.

"Oooh Lord! What the fuck he do now?" Ghost said, shaking his head.

"What happened?"

"Man, Me, Greatness, Stretch, and them was balling at the park. We were playing some niggas from Rockview for a couple dollars. As usual we was beating their ass, and once it was time to get paid they got on some bullshit."

"Hmmm." Once Demi realized that was all Ghost was going to say, he continued.

"So Greatness took off on the dude, Jay and I followed up. You already know how shit can get. It ended up being a big free for all."

"And? Y'all little niggas always fighting them Rock-view niggas."

"I know, but then, Black pulled out a strap and ....."

"What? Who did what?" Asked Ghost.

"The nigga 'Black' backed-out on us."

"Little Black from the Tre?"

"Yeah, him. And you already know Greatness. He's not trying to let it go."

Ghost just shook his head.

"When y'all gonna learn?"

"Ghost, it wasn't our fault. They got on some bullshit first."

"How much?"

Demi was a little confused by this question.

"How much what?"

"How much did y'all bet on the game?"

"Like $100 a piece." Said Demi.

Ghost chuckled. *"A $100! So y'all ready to crash out over a petty-ass $100"*

"It wasn't about the money..."

"I know, I know. They tried to play y'all. They disrespected y'all. Demi, you too smart to be so dumb."

Demi just stared at Ghost.

Ghost let out a sigh of frustration

"Demi, you have to wise up. Every time I turn around, you're in some bullshit."

"It wasn't my ..." Demi said.

"I know, it wasn't your fault, it was Greatness'." Ghost held up his hand to stop Demi from arguing.

"Just think about it little homie .... Think about all the shit that you been involved in over the last couple of years. Now, tell me how many times were you the cause of them. How many times could they have been avoided if it wasn't for Greatness being Greatness? I keep telling you, your man is going to get you locked up or worse case, killed! You're never gonna be able to touch no serious money with Ol' boy on your hip. But hey, you grown. You'll learn...."

"Learn what?" Sade asked, as she entered the room and gave them their plates.

"Where running around with that fool, Greatness is going to get him." Sade sat down on the love seat across from them and crossed her legs, exposing her beautiful brown thighs, hypnotizing a young Demi G.

"Ghost, stop being hard on Demi G and Greatness. You were the same with Tone when you were younger." Sade told Ghost.

"Yeah, and it got my ass 5 years, almost more. Then I cut his dumb-ass off."

"Yeah ..... afterwards. But, it took you a while to see Tone for what he was before you cut him off." Sade said, making a valuable point.

"I know baby, but it almost cost me my life. I just don't want Demi to find out the hard way like I did."

Demi just sat and listened as Ghost and Sade conversed about him as if he wasn't even there.

"You know damn well Greatness ain't nothing, but trouble." Sade got up, leaving the love seat and sat between Ghost and Demi. She turned towards Ghost, placing her hand on his thigh.

"I know baby, but sometimes we have to go through the fire and get burned to learn. All you can do is advise and be patient. And you ....."

Sade turned towards Demi G. When she did, Demi G's eyes went wide as he caught a glimpse of her neatly trimmed pussy before she re-crossed her legs, adjusted her robe and took Demi G's hands into hers.

"And you.... You know how Ghost feels about you, and you know he would never tell you anything wrong."

"I know but, Greatness...." Said Demi

"You don't know nothing. All you know about that boy is that he can fight and play basketball."

"I know he always got my back." Demi G said, defending his friend.

"Okay granted, but does it outweigh the fact that he keeps you in some shit? So, when you're doing 30 years because you got caught up in his bull-shit, and your mom is crying because her baby is gone and she's heart broken."

Demi G didn't know what to say so he just listened.

"Demi, you're smart. I thought you wanted to be a lawyer, so you could help our people. What happened to that?"

"I still do."

"How are you gonna do that when every other week you're suspended for fighting? Ghost told me that the school said according to their test score on you, they consider you academically gifted."

"Well I'm gonna leave, so y'all two can handle what needs to be handled. Old man, don't be here all day either." Sade smirked, as she walked past Ghost, earning herself a hard slap on the ass.

"I'ma call Dawg and we're gonna meet up with him and Black, y'all little niggas are gonna squash this shit."

"Man Ghost, them niggas....."

"Demi, I said y'all gonna squash that shit." Ghost looked at Demi. He knew that Ghost was serious. Ghost never raised his voice whenever he got angry. His voice always got extremely low.

"I'm not gonna let y'all start no dumb-ass beef over no fucking basketball game. Bodies dropping is always bad for business."

After Ghost got off the phone with Dawg, he had Demi G call Greatness.

"Hello..."

"What's up, Greatness?"

"Chilling, what's up with you?"

"Hanging with Ghost. He wants us to squash that shit with Black."

"Naw man, fuck that! That nigga pulled out a strap on us. Man I'm at that nigga's head soon as I see him." Ghost could hear Greatness screaming through his phone so he took it from Demi G.

"Shorty you listen to me, that shit is dead."

"Ghost man ....."

"That shit is dead!"

35

Ghost was very serious about conveying his message to young Greatness. *"You about to start a war over some basketball game? Over a punk-ass $100?"*

"It's a Man, ain't nobody scared of Black and them."

"Fuck Black! What do you think Dawg is gonna do if you kill his little man? He's gonna fuck your whole world up. He's not gonna play with you. On sight, whenever he sees you; with your girl, mom, it doesn't matter!"

"I'm not scared of that nigga Dawg either. He might got all y'all old heads shook but..."

"You're dumber than I thought. Who the fuck is talking about being scared? I'm talking about making the strip hot, fucking a nigga's money up, getting a nigga a rack of time. There's a lot of nigga in the graveyard that wasn't scared." Ghost stopped to catch his breath.

"Ghost man, look, I hear you old man but....."

"But nothing. Greatness, I called Dawg already and told him to meet us. We're gonna meet them niggas, squash this shit and that's what it is."

When Greatness didn't respond, Ghost asked him.

"Did you hear what I said?"

"Yeah, aiight. When you trying to meet up?"

"Meet us out the way on Wilmont Rd. in an hour."

"Yeah, aiight."

When Greatness hung up, Ghost looked at Demi G and shook his head. "Go ahead and finish your food while I get dressed. That little nigga is crazy. I'm telling you Demi, ease up on him before it's too late."

Demi G didn't respond, so Ghost just shook his head once more, and went to get dressed.

Chapter Three

Dawg and Black were sitting down talking when Ghost and Demi G pulled up, and hopped out of a 1996 midnight blue Acura Legend.

"Joey Ghost, what's good my nigga?"

"Dawg, what's happening? Black, what's up with you little homie?"

"Ain't shit Dawg, how're you old head?"

"I'm good lil bro. Black told me about y'all situation earlier. That shit should've never gotten that far. But shit happens. Nobody got hurt so it shouldn't be no problem for y'all to move pass this shit, right?"

"Me and Black cool, I don't have no beef with him."

"That's what's up. I'm glad to hear that, y'all two shake hands and let that shit go."

Demi G and Black did as Dawg said.

Moments later, they all spotted Greatness coming up the Hill from the Brookside projects direction. The West Rock neighborhood has the surrounding projects. Rockview circle is basically situated at the top the Hill. It's separated by a wooded area from Westville manor.

Greatness rode up on a Bmx trick bike. He had on, some basic blue jeans and a black hoodie.

"Greatness, what's up bro?" Demi asked, as he gave Greatness some dap.

"Ain't nothing, Demi. What's good, Ghost? What's up, Dawg?" Purposely leaving out Black, greeting the O.G.'s. Black just chuckled.

"Greatness, stop with the bullshit. We just talked about this shit on the phone." Ghost said in exasperation.

"That whole situation was about nothing."

"Nothing! That nigga pulled out on me in front of everybody." Greatness said, with extreme rage in his tone.

"Shorty, fuck them little niggas. Nobody ain't going to remember that shit a week from now. Y'all motherfuckas fight all the time." Dawg added, trying to talk some sense into Greatness.

"Greatness, I got no beef with you. Shit happens. If the shoe was on the other foot, and your homies were getting fucked up, and you had a burner on you; what would you have done?" Black asked, as he walked up to Greatness.

"We wouldn't be having this conversation because I would have popped y'all niggas." Greatness responded, looking Black in the eyes.

For a moment, nobody said anything, the two wolves just stared at each other.

"That's good to know. Maybe I'll just do that next time." Black fired back.

"It's not going to be a next time." Ghost said, he stepped in between the two.

"That's what I'm saying. Y'all gonna let that shit go and dead it right here, right now. we're not asking y'all, we're telling y'all." Dawg growled, tired of the kid games.

Greatness and Black stared at each other for a few moments longer before Ghost barked.

"Greatness!" Greatness looked at Ghost, then said …. *"Yeah, aight, that shit is dead."*

"Black, Demi?"

"That shit is dead Dawg." Both of them responded.

"Alright then. Damn y'all little niggas are crazy." Ghost laughed at Dawg.

"Dawg, ain't no way we were this bad at their age."

"Hell no! These crazy little motherfuckers don't care about nothing, but their pride and ego." Dawg responded to Ghost's statement.

"They don't care about getting money, going to jail, getting pussy, ..."

"Hold up, Ghost, I can't speak for Demi and Greatness; but I definitely care about pussy." Everyone laughed at Black, even Greatness cracked a smile.

"Alright then, if we all cool, I gotta bounce. Me and my lady are still celebrating my B-day."

"Oh shit, Happy birthday bro." Everybody followed Dawg's lead and congratulated Ghost on making it through another year.

"Appreciated, appreciated. I'll get up with you later, Dawg. Black fall back and be easy. Focus a little more on that pussy."

"I got you O.G." Black answered, laughing. He dapped Demi and Greatness, then turned to see what Dawg was going to get into. They started walking towards Dawg's Benz. Greatness stared, walking in the same direction just as Ghost was about to ask him if he was good and see if he wanted a ride.

"Ayo, you straight little..... Greatness." Greatness ignored Ghost, as he continued walking.

"What's up with him?" Ghost asked Demi G.

"He's probably still mad. He'll be alright, A....Greatness." Greatness was about 6 feet away from Dawg's car when Demi G called his name.

By the time Dawg and Black were both sitting in the car, Greatness had drawn his 17 shot P-89 Ruger. He pointed his 9mm at Black and smiled .... squeezing off 8 shots right through the passenger side of the windshield, striking Black all in his upper body.... Then turned toward Dawg's direction, firing, emptying the rest of the clip into his Benz. Without hesitating, he looked at Demi G and Ghost; and said, "That's how you call the shots. Now niggas know about pulling out guns and not busting!"

"What the fuck, Greatness ...... You just started everything that we were trying to prevent. All over your fucking pride." Ghost said, furiously.

"Ghost, fuck those pussy-ass niggas and whoever else that's not with us! They can get it too ..... Period!" Greatness said, without blinking.

"Damn, I guess this shit just got real.... But, on some real nigga shit you could've used your head bro." Demi G asked his right-hand man.

"Now, I'm straight." Greatness said, pedaling off slowly on his bike as if nothing just happened.

Ghost and Demi got in the Acura, looked at each other, then pulled off from the scene. They sat in silence for few minutes until Ghost stopped at a red light. He slammed his hands against the steering wheel.

"Fuck, shit.... What I tell you about that young dumba muthafuc..."

"O.G., calm down, we just got to come up with a plan because this shit about to get ugly fast!" Knowing deep down inside that his man, Greatness, had really violated this time and was getting out of control. With that, Demi G still couldn't see himself not coming to the aid of his best friend, no matter if he was in the wrong.

"So what's the plan? I have my Davenport posse on deck, ready for all the smoke, and you already know them Segal st. niggas always ready to ride and stand on the business."

"I should kill that little dumb muthafucka." Said Ghost.

"Dawg was a real good nigga. He was solid, and his reach was just as long as mine."

"What do you mean was? We don't know for a fact that Dawg and Black are dead yet, maybe they just got hit up bad." Demi G said, making a valid point.

"Na.... ain't no way them nigga survived all them shots. There was too much blood."

Ghost witnessed a lot in his day. As much as he hoped Dawg and Black were alive, he knew that they were better off dead.

"So, you know niggas ain't gonna lay down or sweep this shit under the rug." Ghost knew he had some major problems on his hands. He knew that if it came out that Greatness was the one who slaughtered Dawg and Black, he had a war on his hands. Anyone that was associated with him could possibly become a target.

"I'm not gonna lie, Demi G. This shit just put us all in a bad predicament."

"Call both cliques to my spot in an hour, and I do mean everyone."

Chapter Four

GREATNESS

"Say word cuz that you did not just do no shit like that in front of the O.G. Ghost and Demi G. You know the streets are about to get ugly with Dawg gone. He was the O.G. to all them Tre niggas, and everyone had mad love for Black little crazy ass."

"Greatness, you already know we're on whatever time you're on bro, but what did O.G. Ghost say?" asked Nasty.

Nasty was another young wild killer from the Hill that always shot first and never asked any questions later. His right-hand man was Lunatic, whose name speaks for itself and needs no explanations!

Both of their loyalty belonged to Greatness, and despite Greatness' reckless actions, they were on board for all the bullshit.

"First and foremost, Fuck Dawg and Black! Black wanted to play a big boy game, so I put his ass down! Plus, them Tre niggas had to know that I wasn't letting that shit go. I wasn't letting that nigga Black get one up on me."

Greatness understood the value of a threat, and Black was most definitely a threat.

"As far as Demi G, he's my dog, he would never leave me standing alone. I know he doesn't like the play I picked, but fuck it, we here now! Feel me, Nasty?"

Ring, ring, ring …...

Greatness looked down at his Motorola phone, and saw that it was Ghost calling. Shaking his head, thinking himself, *"Speaking of the devil."*

"What's up, O.G?"

"We are all meeting at my spot now, both cliques."

"Cool, we'll be there in 10 minutes."

Even though Greatness had the utmost respect for all of the old heads in his hood, he still didn't like being told what to do, ever! He hated authority.

"Damn, that was the big homie"

"Yeah? Come on Lunatic, we got a meeting."

- - -

- 20 minutes later -

"I appreciate y'all for coming here at such short notice. For those that don't know why I called for this meeting, it's due to one of our own doing something so stupid out of pride and emotions. We are at war with the entire Tre, thanks to Greatness. But that's not important.... What is important is that everyone in

46

this room must be on point from here on, out and always be
strapped. Point, blank, period!"

Ghost looked around the room at all his young soldiers. Ready
for war!

Nasty, Lunatic, Bay-Bay, Wildboy, Dog, Star, Buck, Cannon,
Lee, Demi G, and Greatness all sat there at attention.

"Because we don't really know how many people knew
about us meeting with Dawg and Black; or how many people
saw that fight Greatness and Demi G had at the basketball court,
or who just might try and put two-and-two together. So, we must
keep our ears to the streets and stay
on point. This shit is not a game, bodies going to be dropping.
Also, we have to worry about the police, they're another problem.
So, let's try to stay as low as possible. And as for making this
money, it won't be easy with all the extra heat on the
streets......"

"Oh shit! Look O.G., on the TV......"

- - -

- Breaking News -

Just in on News Channel 8. *"We're here on the scene of a double*
shooting in the West Rock neighborhood. We've been told by the
Chief of the NHPD that there isn't much information that he can
share at this time. It has been reported that the two men who

were shot here today have just been pronounced dead at the scene. New Haven detectives believe that the crime was drug related. A drug deal gone wrong. The two victims whose identities are being withheld until the families are notified, were found shot multiple times in a 2002 gray Mercedes Benz. Detectives on the scene discovered in the trunk of the vehicle 18 kilos of cocaine which holds an estimated street value of $ 900,000."

"Police are asking for anyone who might have information to this double homicide to please contact the crime stoppers hotlines at 1-800-crime stoppers. This is Kelly Jones signing off."

"Damn.... 18 bricks!"

"That can't be all you just heard, Greatness. You have to be smarter than that." Said Ghost.

"First of all, fuck them niggas. They're DEAD!"

"Yes, you made sure of that, didn't you?"

"You got something you want to get off your chest, Demi G?"

"Yea nigga! As a matter of fact, I do! That shit was dumb and reckless...... you've been my man since I can remember, but that still don't mean I have to agree with all the decisions you make. A real friend tells their homie when they're in the wrong, or do some dumb shit. Now where does this leave

us as brotherhood? You're my dog till the wheels fall off, but this shit is much bigger than you.... Shit, it's bigger than the both of us put together. Do you care for anyone in this room? Or just yourself? Bro, because of your pride and emotions, you put all of us in a fucked-up situation."

This was one of the things Greatness loved and hated about Demi G. He always spoke his mind and made good sense...... which still didn't mean he had to like it......but he did respect it.

"Man, I care about everybody in this room, but at the end of the day, I'm not tolerating no disrespect from anyone."

"Well, my question is we really don't know who's gonna come out and play on Dawg and Black's behalf. All I'm saying is be on point, and be ready for whoever and whatever comes our way."

"Dawg had connections and alliances with a bunch of individuals throughout the entire city. He was a major player in the game, which means niggas are going to be out for blood! So again......all of us need to be prepared and ready for whatever these streets have in store for us, period."

For a young boy, Demi G most definitely possessed all the qualities and potential it took to be a true boss. He was the brains of his entire crew. Majority of all the young niggas from around his neighborhood respected and valued his words and opinion. One of his favorite sayings he always recited was, "Intelligence over emotions" …... Emotions can take you places but intelligence will take you where you want to be.

Ghost knew Demi G had all the right influence over the young niggas.

"We'll make sure y'all move in pairs of two because them Tre niggas will be out head-hunting in these streets……oh yeah, before I forget, I will be through to collect the bread later on for re-up, so be ready." Ghost said.

"Big homie, you really think it's a good idea to be trying to get more work at a time like this?" Demi G asked.

"Dawg is gone. So the market just got a little bigger. There aren't many that can supply the clientele that Dawg had. That extra paper is going to be floating around……. So we are going to grab it! Point, blank, period!"

"Understood! Well shit, I got to study for S.A.T… D.P.P., we out of here." Shouted Demi G.

"Segal street, let's bounce and get to this money." Said Greatness.

"Well, y'all be on point out there."

"Safety…… O.k. Ghost."

Chapter Five

Ghost stood at the bottom of his stairs and watched everybody leave out of his basement. He was standing there in deep thought when his moment of peace was interrupted by ...

"So, I guess Greatness done did some dumb shit again, huh?" Sade asked, concerned about her man. She knew whenever Ghost was quiet in his thoughts, something wasn't right, and normally when that happens someone was going to get hurt.

"Yes, my love......He definitely put us in a fucked-up situation. So I'ma need you to pack a bag and go down to the ranch house in P.A. for a little while just until shit cool down."

"What?"

"Nigga, you must be crazy if you think I'm going to P.A. to be all alone in that big-ass ranch house."

"First of all, Sade, I don't remember me asking you a damn thing. I'm telling yo ass to go pack you some shit. Now, go and just do as I say!"

Sade could see the frustration growing on her man's face, but at the moment she couldn't give a flying fuck. She had no intentions on going to P.A...

"First of all, my ass! Nigga watch your mouth! I'm not one of your little niggas that just left. So please, Joey, watch how you

handle me, okay? Why would you think for a second that I would even be comfortable with just going and leaving you anywhere near all of this bullshit?"

Sade was trying her best to convince Ghost to allow her to stay in town with him, knowing that there were dark clouds on the way over the city. Shit was about to get ugly.

"Baby, listen to me ...... I'm not trying to be mean or piss you off, but this shit ain't up for negotiation. Now go pack your stuff. You're going, and that's that!" Ghost demanded.

"So, let me ask you a question? Who's going to have your back like me, huh? A bunch of little niggas you're always taking care of? Huh? Let me help you answer that question...... Fuck NO!"* Said Sade, moving her head side to side; letting her inner chicken head manifest a little.

"What did you just say to me? Watch you fucking mouth b ...."

"Say it nigga! I dare you!"

"Don't you ever talk about them like that! Those same little niggas are part of the reason you're living the way you do now!" All that Gucci and Fendi ain't cheap! We wouldn't be where we're without them."

Ghost walked to the bottom of the stairs, pulling Sade close to his body.

"Listen Queen.... I know for sure that you'll always have a nigga's back, and best interest at heart without a doubt. But you're just going to have to trust me..."

"My intentions are to keep you safe, and out of harm's way; you being here will just distract me. I can't be fully focused in these streets with you around. I'ma be worried-sick. I can't afford to be slipping right now."

"But baby I can take care of myself. You know that."

"Yes, Sade, I know and understand you can; but I don't know what I would do if something happens to you." Said Ghost, with the utmost compassion in his voice.

"So, how do you think I would feel if something happens to you? I would be crushed!" Said Sade, making Ghost feel bad. Ghost paused for a few seconds.......

"O.K.., since I see that we're not getting anywhere with this situation, I'ma meet you halfway. You can stay in town, but you're staying with the young homie, Demi G, at his crib; so, at least I'll know that you'll be out of the line of fire. But, I want you to play the house, you understand me?"

"Yes Ghost", Sade screamed in excitement.

"I'm being serious, Sade. If I catch your ass even on the porch you're gone to P.A., got it?"

"Yes baby."

- - -

- On Demi G Steps -

"Damn, this is some bullshit! I can't believe Greatness did some stupid shit like that in the first place, so now the entire Hill is at war from North to South."

"Yeah Lee, I know this is some bullshit, but we're here now. What is done is done."

Lee was a spitting image of Bruce Lee. He was half-black and Korean with curly hair. Lee was only 7 years old when his mother was murdered by her pimp, which just happened to be his father. His father was convicted of 1st degree murder, and sentenced to 64 years in prison.

Lee became a ward of the state, and was thrown into the foster care system. His only family was Demi G and the rest of the D.P.P. crew. He would go to hell and back for them.

"Yeah, but war brings no money homie." Said Lee.

"That's a fact. That's why I came up with a plan. We all push from 6 a.m. to 5 p.m. hard. Then after 5, we shut down, playing all the back streets like West and Thorn street after dark to people out our business. Now, every other day, we'll rotate switching shifts from 3 p.m. to 12 a.m.....3 days out of the week, we lay low and put shit to bed." Demi G created a set schedule for his entire crew.

"Lee, listen little bro, shit is bout to turn up out here, so be on point and don't ever make yourself a sitting duck! Understood?" Lee shook his head.

"And the same goes for the rest of you."

"Yeah, came from the entire crew."

"So, three days out of the week, we'll be on the bullshit. Head-hunting! I'm talking early mornings and late nights."

"We gonna strike first......No questions asked! You see an op......You shoot an op."

"Now, my question is, does anyone have a problem with anything I just said? Speak now or forever hold your peace."

"I have a question." Said Cannon.

Cannon was another wild young one from Davenport. He was nice with the heat, he couldn't read or write, but when it came to guns, he could tell you about them joints inside and out.

"What are the chances of us making it through this shit in one piece is what I'm asking?" Cannon asked Demi G.

"Well bro, this is pistol waving New Haven.....So, nothing is promised. I know for a fact that we all have our weaknesses, myself included. We play ball, we're fly, and we're some young hustling muthafuckas. But in life, evolution is necessary."

55

Demi G knew deep down that him and his crew had to become ruthless, and put in some pain so the streets wouldn't have any choices, but to respect them.

Chapter Six

Introduction of Chuyloco

Chuyloco was from Lubbock, Texas, better known as the Hub-City for its railroad tracks built in the late 1800's. Every train that run in Texas had to, at some point in time, come through Lubbock station.

Chuyloco was an illegal immigrant born in Mexico. He came to the United States, on the run, from a rival Cartel. Chuy always kept his ties to his Cartel, and been flooding the U.S. with the purest cocaine since the late 1980's.

Chuy and his crew needed to set up a shop somewhere near the northeast, and felt that Connecticut was the perfect place to move his product. One day, in the summertime, downtown in New Haven; Chuy spotted a young well-dressed man in an Armani two-piece suit carrying what looked like a very expensive briefcase made by Louis Vuitton. The man had a lawyer type of look.

"Hey, excuse me young man."

"Hello, how may I help you Sir?" Demi G responded.

"My name is Jose. I'm not from around here and I'm looking for a lawyer to represent one of my young guys. Can you help me?" Said Chuy.

Demi G just thought to himself, *"I'm just an intern, not really a lawyer yet ..."*

"Look sir, I'm not a real lawyer, I'm going to school at Yale University, majoring in criminal justice, but I think I can point you in the right direction for legal assistance." Demi G handed Chuy his card.

"I really appreciate you, Mr. Edwards." Chuy was reading the name off the card Demi G just handed him.

"You are welcome, sir. One thing that I know for sure, nowadays, law enforcement agencies are corrupt."

Demi G asked Jose. *"So, what are the charges your young guys are being held on?"*

"Oh, he just got caught with about two kilos on south I-95 going to Bridgeport." Chuy said.

"Damn !!!" Demi G said to himself, *"two kilos? I know there's more where that came from."*

What Chuyloco didn't know was that Demi G was far from just a college student; he was a cold gangsta and ran one of the most notorious crews out of the Hill, better known as D.P.P.

"Was it raw coke, or was it cooked up?" Demi asked.

"Nah, it was raw coke." Said Chuy.

"O.k., so the feds might be interested in this. Alright, first of all, is he Mexican?"

"No, no, no…… He's a white boy from Guildfort, Ct."

"O.k., so I was going to say if the Feds were to pick this up, minimum, because his offense would be 500 or more grams if it was coke, 50 or more grams of bass/crack would trigger a 10-year mandatory minimum to life." Demi G said.

"Since he's white, they might not look to indict him, he would probably receive probation."

"Nowadays, getting caught with 2 keys would still alarm the Feds. I know you've been watching the news. All the killings and gang activities that's been happening in New Haven has the Feds on high alert. 9 out of 10 times, the feds are going to put 2-and-2 together, just because he was coming through New Haven."

"Well, I got all the money to make this go away Mr. Edwards." Chuy said.

"Listen Mr. Jose, I'm an intern for one of the biggest law firms in Elm City, but this doesn't take any of the heat off you, sir!"

Chuy shook his head, telling himself that he knew Mr. Edwards was right, and thought for the right price he could have the case fly into thin air and disappear.

"Look Mr. Jose, my advice to you is to lay low until this blows over, and pray to God the white boy don't fold." Said Demi G.

Demi G was also praying the white boy didn't fold because he needs Jose. This could turn out to be an opportunity of a lifetime, meeting a Mexican with a lot of weight. Demi G felt this was the jackpot he needed.

"Look Mr. Jose, give me a call as soon as possible. I'm going to holla at the law firm I work at to look into this case for you, but in the meantime, please lay low and don't speak to anyone about this, sir." Demi G said, looking into the eyes of Chuy.

"O.K Mr. Edwards, you're right, I will call you tomorrow. At noon?"

"Yes sir, perfect, that's my lunch break. I'll be waiting on your call." Said Demi G.

Demi G was thinking to himself about hurrying back to Davenport to put out more packs to his crew, then call Greatness to tell him about his encounter with Jose and how their lives probably just changed.

As Chuyloco walked away, he looked back at Mr. Edwards and knew that he was a street dude. Everything about Mr. Edwards smelled 'street'. He was intelligent, and moved like a real gangster. The big mystery was why in the hell did he want to be a lawyer? Chuy's mind continued wondering.

- - -

- Nue -

"Damn nigga! This dick is big as fuck! It seems like it grew since the last time I saw this dick." Nue was thinking to herself as she was sucking Demi G's dick.

"Damn baby, you going hard baby." Demi G said, while guiding her head up and down on his dick. Nue is from a project called the Tribe. The Tribe is known for robbing niggas, so they're always beefing with other neighborhoods. Nue was one of the few that made it out due to her being so beautiful. She was pretty, slim, around 5'10 and extremely intelligent. She began a modeling career, finding herself on the front cover of all the high and top magazines from here to Paris. She always scheduled time to come back home to visit her family, and of course to see her first love, Demi G.

When Demi G and Nue were younger, they used to always sneak to fool around, due to the beef between Hill and The Tribe. Demi G never stepped foot in The Tribe, and Nue never came to the Hill because all his niggas used to say, *"Demi G don't let that pussy get you smoked."*

"Damn baby, I always tell you to let me know when you're about to bust, elk!!" Nue said.

"And why does it seem like you have extra cum coming out? You need to go see a doctor. This isn't normal."

"How the fuck you know what normal is? You always told me that I'm the only nigga you been fucking" said Demi G, with a funny look on his face

"Baby, yes you are, I hate when you act like I'm lying about just fucking you. You already know that I play with my pussy when I'm watching porn. That's how I know about other niggas nutting." Nue was lying through her teeth with a straight face, a performance worthy of winning an academy award. Nue knew she had her body count up since her career took off. Knowing she been fucking other niggas like rappers and other celebrities. Demi G knew Nue was lying, and he also knew when he bust a nut, it wasn't normal because all the female he fucked said the exact same thing to him.

"But anyway baby, we need to talk about you and your girlfriend, Mary."

"What is her issue?" Nue asked.

"I heard she still ain't gave no pussy, talking about she's still a virgin ...No, she ain't!" Said Nue.

Nue couldn't stand the fact that Demi G was in love with Mary, who was a well-known whore to everyone, but Demi G.

"She's been fucking my cousin, Maineball, that's from my hood. That nasty bitch been fucking behind your back since Hill House. Now that y'all not in school anymore, she can become a full-time whore." Nue was going hard but she was telling the truth about Mary.

Mary is Brown-skinned, 5'3 and beautiful, the whole school was on her body.

Demi G heard numerous rumors about Mary fucking older dudes that had money, but every time he went to ask her, she'd deny it; but right now, Nue was crushing his heart with this one. Demi G didn't reach, trying his best to show Nue that he cared.

"Nigga keep ya head up." Said Nue. *"How the fuck you going to be pussy-whipped, and you ain't even had the pussy yet?"* Nue laughed.

"I was on the phone with your mother last week, she said you are doing so good in Yale, and that you have a job being an intern at a law firm. You need to really leave streets alone and your boy, Greatness."

Demi G was not trying to hear anything about needing to leave his right-hand man, Greatness, alone.

"Rumor has it that Greatness killed Black and Dawg over $100. He killed some official Tre niggas and someone gotta answer for that...listen Nue...that's my nigga! Wherever he goes, I go!!! Period!" Demi G said.

"But, over $100 though?" asked Nue.

"Listen......it wasn't over no $100; you can't believe everything you hear."

Demi G knew who Nue was receiving her info from. She was getting it from niggas from around her way, because Tribe niggas are allies with the Tre. They call themselves "T.N.T" (Tre N Tribe.)

"I know about T.N.T. Those Tribe niggas can get it just like them Tre niggas." Demi G stood up and said.

"Baby all this is nonsense. We talked about how reckless Greatness is in the past. I just don't want nothing to happen to you because of something Greatness did." Nue got up and sat beside Demi G, and kissed him on his cheek and started stroking his manhood.

"Baby lay back, it's time for me to make you feel better zaddy!" Nue had to hurry and go see the rest of her family before her trip back to Paris.

Demi G was in deep thought about Greatness and how he couldn't control him anymore. All year long, the Tre beef had both hood on fish grease. It seemed every other day, if not everyday, somebody was getting shot. It was difficult for Demi to focus strictly on school! Nue got on top of Demi G and rode him to sleep. She knew she just added fuel to his stress, but she loved him and prayed that he would be one of the ones to make it out of the mean streets of the Elm City.

Chapter Seven

Joey Ghost...

"Ayo Champ, recount this money. I think it's short."

"Short......Short by what?" Champ asked.

"$12,000....... Damn! That's not a short, that's half a chicken" said Champ, referring half a chicken to half a brick.

"Yea, it's supposed to be $86,000, not $74,000." Ghost explained.

"Ayo call Messy, tell him this shit is way too short and to go back to the hood to collect the rest of my money from them little niggas that be on Hamilton side. I always got issues with those little-crazy muthafuckas." Said Ghost.

"Franklin St. niggas always come correct and we all from the same projects. Let's get this money cuz."

Ghost gave Champ their hood dap. Clapping his hand twice, then throwing up their project sign to their chest. Joey Ghost is originally from Franklin St. projects, also known as the "Ghetto." The nickname was jacked from the Ghetto Boys in the early 90's.

Joey Ghost is the supplier of coke in almost every neighborhood. He got about 6 hoods in a headlock. He supplies West Hills, The Hill, The Ville, Tre, Fair Haven and Ansonia. Even though

Ansonia is just a small town right outside of the Elm City, it's considered a hood to the Elm. They get the same amount of respect as if Ansonia was just a name of a hood in New Haven.

"Big bro, them little niggas ain't picking up the phone. They had to fuck that bread up!" Said Messy.

Messy was a short cocky nigga that kept two XD-40 Cals on him at all times; he's always WAR READY! He worked for Ghost and also Joey Ghost's adopted son. Messy's mother and father were dope fiends, and didn't give two fucks about their son. So, for years Ghost took Messy in, under his wing.

"Just give me the word, Ghost. I been waiting to fuck them Hamilton niggas up, especially T-Nice." Said Messy.

"Look little bro, chill the fuck out, you always ready to just go." Ghost said.

"Ayo Ghost, this little nigga is crazy!" Champ chuckled.

"How many times are we going to allow them to keep coming short?" Messy stated.

"Messy, they always paid up. It could just be a misunderstanding, that's all bro." Ghost said.

"Anyway, I gotta go drop this bird off to Demi G on Davenport Ave. I got to go deal with those hot-headed niggas over there, especially Greatness. He's always on some dumb shit!"

"I like Demi G a lot, but he loves Greatness to death. He's going to be his downfall. The nigga, Greatness killed them niggas, Dawg and Lil Black, right in front of my face. That little-reckless nigga got our alliance with Tre on ice; so, personally I feel some type of way. The shit that really make a nigga look crazy between them little niggas. It just makes it look like I orchestrated the whole play for them niggas to get smoked by Greatness." Ghost said, shaking his head. *"Over a $100."*

"Yes, I heard." Said Champ.

- - -

- Greatness -

"Lunatic, wassup lil bro?"

"Us……Never them ……… Segal St. ……. Or beat ya feet ……… And fuck anybody who's against that, period!" Lunatic said, looking into the eyes of Greatness like a straight soldier.

"Ayo look cuz, I was hollering at Rickita the other day and she says she knows some niggas from West Haven that's supposed to be getting some real money." Said Greatness.

"Rickita who?" Lunatic asked.

"Rickita nigga……that's from the Jungle with the wild, crazy fat-ass that run the Candy Girls."

"Ooohhhh shit……. Her ass be jiggling like she got two midgets slap boxing in her jeans?" Greatness said, cracking up laughing.

Lunatic said, *"Yeah, yeah that's her."* While in a daze.

"Okay nigga, snap back Luna!" Said Greatness.

"She seen them clown-ass niggaz counting out about $100,000, so let me know and I'll set the play up A.S.A.P., big bro." Luna said.

"I'm still doing my homework; Rickita don't want it coming back to her at all, and I gotta pay that bitch $20,000 for the lick."

Chapter Eight

Rickita

"Get that money, bitch." Rickita said to one of her hookers that brought her a large bag back.

"Yeah, this a whole week worth of fucking." Evelyn said.

"O.k. then, Candy Girls getting the bag, it should be about $15,000 in that Gucci bag." Kita said.

"It doesn't matter, we gotta count it anyway, Dollar-for-dollar." Kita said.

Evelyn thought to herself, *"This thirsty-ass bitch is all about money with her big stanking ass!"*

"So, where the rest of the hoes?" Rickita asked.

"They still in the projects." Evelyn said.

"In the projects!!!" Kita screamed out.

"Them hoes supposed to be in the whorehouse on Elliot St., getting to a check. Candy Girls don't take breaks, we chase! We chase all day, all fucking day, period!!!" Rickita was upset about her hoes.

"Every time they go to the jungle, these bitches went to party, drink, smoke, do pills and fuck for free! I'ma smack fire out of every one of them dumb bitches." Said Kita.

"As soon as I'm done here in Ansonia, I'm taking my ass to the projects, and I better not see any of them. If I do...They better stay their asses in those projects right where I found them in the first place."

The Candy Girls are originally from the Jungle, which is the projects on Church Street South, located in the Hill neighborhood.

It always been talked about if the jungle was actually part of the Hill or not. You had some that said the Jungle was its own section, and some that say the jungle is part of the Hill.

It is a fact that the jungle is in the Hill neighborhood, but either way, Congress Ave. is the heart of the Hill, and if you went against that, then you go against the entire Hill.

Candace A.K.A. Killa, ran the Candy Girls back in the late 1980's. Selling drugs, pussy, catching robberies, etc., you name it. Candy Girls had a part in it.

Killa was a ruthless cold-blooded Killa. Her name spoke for itself. She went down for a double homicide back in the day, but only got 20 years for it. She pled out in self-defense for the murders, but was found guilty for possession of two illegal military firearms.

Rickita is Killa's little cousin that is from the Jungle. She was very young when Killa got locked up. She kept the Candy-Girl name alive. She always felt she was a Candy Girl, so, she started her own crew. A new version of the infamous Candy Girls. Her crew was known for putting in work. See, Rickita didn't sell pussy, she just made niggas think they were about to get some ass, then talked them right out their money after fucking one of her hookers.

"When I was in West Haven a few days ago on Canton St., one of them corny-ass niggas was counting a lot of money."

"What's a lot of money?" Kita said.

"About $100,000." Evelyn said.

Damn, so, these niggas getting to a bag. It's more where that came from. Rickita was thinking of herself.

"How often do they call you to come over?" Rickita asked.

"Like once a week." Evelyn responded.

"O.K., these niggas are stupid!" Rickita shook her head, saying, *"Tell me more about it."*

"O.K., hold that thought... I'ma make a call real-quick to one of my guys about this." Said Rickita.

"Greatness, how you doing, baby?"

"Who the fuck is this?" Said Greatness.

"This is Kita nigga.......Candy-Girl Kita."

"Oh shit, my bad baby girl, sorry about that." Said Greatness.

"We need to talk a.s.a.p." Kita told him.

"O.K., we can make this happen, give me a time and place tomorrow."

"How about 3.p.m. at Coov Crib on Congress and West?" Rickita suggested.

"Perfect." Greatness said.

"Oh yeah, bring that dark, tall, and handsome Demi G with you."

"Kita, you're always lusting over Demi G. Stop fucking always talking about him every time we talk, Damn." Greatness said.

"Well excuse me, Killa, how else am I supposed to get close to him?" Kita said.

"Look, whatever we do is Segal St. and Candy-Girl business! 3.p.m. tomorrow, Congress and West! BANG!" Said Greatness, hanging up the phone.

"Damn, this nigga is still crazy!" Said Kita

"Look bitch, just finish counting this money, then we're going to the Hill to pick up the rest of the bread from these hoes on Elliot St."

- - -

BLOCKA, BLOCKA, BLOCKA, BLOCKA, BOOM!

"Get the fuck on the ground! This is a stick up!" Plizzy yelled out.

D.P.P. crew put their arms in the sky.

Plizzy and Shellz just ran up on Davenport crew's trap house on the corner of Stevens St. and Davenport Ave. (The Twin Buildings). They blew the hedges off the door with a double barrel sawed-off shotgun, then kicked it down. Of course, they both wore ski masks.

"Run the money, drugs, and jewels!"

Plizzy looked at one of the niggas' feet they were robbing and said, *"Take them Jordans off too."*

"Damn, this is the fourth time this month we been robbed", Ty-Ty was thinking to himself; Demi G ain't going to like this loss-after-loss.

Chapter Nine

Demi G meeting with Chuy

Demi G was riding up State St., going towards Hamden. As soon as he passed the D.M.V., Demi G took a left turn on a real quiet small street. At first, he didn't see anyone, but he was told to just ride up the street and look for the wave. "There goes the wave." Said Demi G.

A real tiny white house. Demi G parked and went to the back yard like he was told.

"Ayo homie, this way." A short Mexican said in a low tone. He followed the Mexican to the back door. Once inside, he was ushered into a room where he met Chuyloco.

"Hey, nice to see you again, Mr. Edwards." Said Chuy.

"Nice to see you again as well, Mr. Jose." Said Demi, knowing that's not his real name.

"Do you have any information for me about my guy?" Chuy asked.

"Yes, I do, sir. The Barnes and Moore law firm that I'm Interning for is asking for $10,000 to retain MR. David Stevens. On the call we had earlier this morning, I told you $20,000, but that changed due to us discovering a loophole. A big one matter of fact."

75

"We discovered that there wasn't any probable cause for the traffic stop, which makes the stop illegal. But there's a catch!" Said Demi G.

"A catch?" Chuy raised his eyebrows.

"Yes, a catch; you see, the thing with this case is that Mr. Stevens had five years hanging over his head from a prior weed case he caught in Guilford."

"So, hold up..." Chuy said.

"But, if he didn't violate any traffic laws, and they claim the stop wasn't legal, shouldn't everything be thrown out?"

"Yes and No!" Demi G said. In the state of Connecticut, the law states that before one can start the process to a suppression hearing or trial, they must first attend a probation hearing of them on papers, which violates his probation stipulations. If found guilty, he will receive the entire five years. The state made him an offer already. Attorney Moore said the lowest and best deal on the table is two years flat with no probation." Demi G explained to the best of his ability.

"2 years huh? This shit sounds like entrapment to me. So, what you're telling me is even though he's innocent due to a technicality, he still got to do time?" Chuy asked.

"Yes sir. Yes, it's a lose-lose situation ... Welcome to the state of Connecticut." Demi G smirked, showing off his pearly white teeth.

"The best thing that could've happened sir, is that no one bonded him out, which means a lot. It will look like a random white boy that just bumped into two kilos instead of being part of a drug organization. His court date for sentencing is set for next month, October 12th, and Mr. Moore said he spoke to one of his friends that is working in the federal court, and they stated that the feds aren't interested in looking into this case." Demi G said.

"Okay, deal!" Chuy went to the closet and grabbed the $20,000 that he already had aside for Demi G, and gave it to him.

"You can give the remaining $10,000 to the Barnes and Moore law firm for the future. A payment for any run-ins that I might have with the law." Chuy said.

"O.K. fine, I got you."

As Demi G was walking out, Chuy said, *"Listen man, we need to talk for a minute."*

"Look, for starters, my name isn't Jose, It's Jesse. The streets know me by Chuy."

"Take a seat here, Mr. Edwards; let me ask you a question......Why do you want to be a lawyer?"

"Ummm, because I'm doing this for my mom, and I want to help the minorities out from the corruption of law enforcement and the government." Demi said.

"Look nigga……cut the bullshit! You ain't no lawyer. I got ears and eyes all over New Haven. You are a straight-gangster from Davenport Ave. over there in the Hill. You're the leader of the notorious D.P.P. crew! Why you keep playing games with me, Demi G?" Chuy said.

"Demi G? I know this nigga was different Damn, he really does have eyes and ears. This nigga just said my street name."

"It wasn't difficult to do my homework on you, Mr. Michael Edwards. Because of your business card, I was able to learn about your mom, friends, girlfriend. Shit! I even know who your connect is…. The one and only, Joey Ghost!" Chuy explained.

"Look, I can see that you want to leave the streets alone…I get it! But the street is in you. You can't hide it, Demi G. it's written all over your face. I can even smell it on your breath."

Demi G put his head down because he knew no matter how hard he tried to conceal who he was, somehow, the true Demi G would always reveal himself.

Demi G was trying his best to play it off, as if he wasn't interested in what Chuy had to say. Demi G thought about how an opportunity like this would change his life overnight. He would be in a position to elevate his whole situation from his soldiers, to the amount of cocaine flooding his hood.

Demi G had a good feeling where this conversation was heading. He wanted to be a part of Chuy's cartel. He would have the Hill on smash...or better yet... The entire Elm City. The only person that would be in the way would be Joey Ghost.... oh yeah, and Greatness wild, wild nut ass!

"Look Demi G, I will make you the richest man on the east coast if you hear me out and fuck with me." Said Chuy, looking Demi G straight in the eyes.

"One thing I hate is street gangs. It brings all types of unwarranted attention and I know you're the leader of D.P.P., low key you might be, but once you're governing a bunch of maniacs, dysfunction is inevitable. Demi G, you have to know when and when not to be selfish." Said Chuy.

"Just recently... My folks, Black and Dawg, were running for me. They had 18 kilos that belonged to me. They were transporting them to one of my spots out West Hills. There was a conflict that they were trying to dead it, but they ended up being the dead ones. All over $100......Sounds familiar?" Asked Chuy.

"The word is, Joey Ghost set them up for your friend, Greatness! Which you were there right?" Demi G positioned his

hand ready to grab his glock-19 out if his holster, but heard,
"Don't try nothing stupid!" Said by one of Chuy's cartel goons.

"I'm all about business my young friend, until you fuck
with my money." Chuy said.

"The whole town knows Greatness is wild, and you can't
control him, but your loyalty for him is real. That's something
that's small. In due time, you'll see Greatness for what he really
is!" Said Chuy.

Chuy knew that the only way it was going to work with Demi G
is that Greatness had to be out of the picture permanently.

"18 Kilos is a big deal for me. That's $360,000 at $20,000
per key." Demi G knew not to say nothing, Joey Ghost taught
him if he ever found himself in this type of situation, just don't
say shit. Demi petrified because he knew at any second, he could
be killed by those crazy-ass Mexicans. $360,000 was a lot of
money. Demi G knows he doesn't have that type of bread, so, he
had no idea where he was going to get the money to pay Chuy
back. All he was thinking about was how once again, he was in a
fucked-up position because of crazy-ass Greatness. Chuy was
dead-quiet for about 3 minutes, watching the fear flow through
the veins of Demi G. Demi G attempted to say something.

"Shut the fuck up!!" Chuy yelled out. Chuy got in the
face of Demi G.

"Listen to me, look me in my eyes when I'm talking to you. This isn't up for negotiation, Demi." Said Chuy.

"I'm going to front you about 40 kilos per month. The going rate for a key is $24,000 in the Elm. My price is $20,000 per kilo. So, I want $24,000 for the first 20 keys, and $20,000 for the remaining 20 keys. The $4,000 off the first 20 keys will go towards the $360,000. That will be $80,000. After that, I will up the shipment to 60 Kilos! Do we have an understanding, Demi?" Chuy asked him, as if he really had a choice.

Demi G was in deep thought like, *"Who the fuck this nigga thinks he talking to? This shit is extortion at its best! I ain't never been a bitch! But, this is a chance of a lifetime. I'm still getting $80,000 a month now, then after the fifth and final month, I'll be getting $200,000. "O.K. Chuy, we got a deal!!"* Demi G said.

"I almost felt that if I didn't agree with you, I was dead."

"We would never know!" Chuy responded, with a devilish smile.

"Take this cell phone. I will be the only person contacting you on this phone."

"Okay, I got you." Demi G said.

"No more petty hustling for you…… it's over."

"I will give you a call on where to go pick up the first shipment." Chuy smiled and told himself, *"My plan is in motion. He will never expect this coming."*

Chapter Ten

Ring, ring, ring, ring.......

"Wassup Ty-Ty?" Demi G said.

"Big bro, I gotta holla at you A.S.A.P., we have been robbed again. This is the fourth time this month. Two times in front of the store Leon's, and now twice in the Twin Buildings."

"Hold on... Chill over the phone, Ty-Ty."

"Where are you right now?" Asked Demi G.

"I'm on Congress Ave. and West, in the projects with Hov, Coov, P.J., and Dada."

"O.k., bet, Call the rest of the posse, Segal St.gang, Congress Ave. brothers, Elliot St. Posse, Sylvan Ave. and Vernon and Ward niggas. Everyone should meet me at 6p.m. in the backyard at Uncle Joes."

"Say no more." Ty-Ty said.

"Shit!! Think I just missed him."

"Who? Missed Who?"

"Dee Gotti." Agent Bob Andrews was telling his partner, Tracy Rose.

"Are you sure it was him?" asked Agent Rose.

"He's in the same blue jeep that our informant said, with the cracked windshield."

The United States government launched an investigation into the Hill criminal activities. Dee Gotti is from Congress Ave. He's part of the Congress Ave. brothers. C.A.B., who has nothing, or no one to be played with. They're notorious for the shootings and murders.

Dee Gotti has been targeted by the United States government on information about drugs and gun sales provided by a reliable informant. Dee Gotti has been on the Feds radar for some time now, almost 10 years to be exact. Dee Gotti is someone you would consider a ghost. He's almost never seen in the daytime. It's damn near-impossible to get close to him. His dealings are strictly for his C.A.B.'s.

Dee Gotti is a little older than Demi G. They became good friends growing up in the neighborhood. Besides his Congress Ave. family, Demi G was the only nigga he trusted outside of the circle.

"We gotta meet our informant about an hour from now." Said Agent Andrews.

"He said it's a big meeting for all Hill North, Demi G called for the meeting. Everyone is expected to attend."

"So do you think it's safe to wire him up now?" Agent Tracy asked.

I don't think it's the right time, we can't afford to have his cover blown. We need him; he's the only person that can get close to Demi G, then we'll be able to get close to the untouchable "Dee Gotti" himself!

"Well, I guess you're right." Said Tracy, while pulling off at Kossuth and Ann St.

- - -

- Greatness -

"Fuck me harder, Zaddy! Bang! Bang! Bang! Damn daddy ...... Ooooo, yesssss! Oooooo shitttt! HARDER......" She was screaming out, while Greatness pounded away, hitting that fat, wet pussy from the back.

"Damn bitch, this pussy is sooooo gooodd! So good, agghhhh!" Greatness released a load inside her.

"Damn, I want to tell you I love you; but, I don't, I love that pussy tho...." They both just laughed, trying to catch their breath.

"Listen ma, I got a meeting to go to. I really don't care about the stupid-ass meeting."

"Why?" She asked

"Because I'm Segal St. gang! Me and my niggas are not about to be part of the Hill anymore." Greatness said.

"But, Demi G is your best friend. He really does love you..."

"Fuck Demi G!!" Greatness shouted out. *"He thinks he run shit, but he doesn't run shit over here. I RUN SHIT!"*

"But baby, why? He is harmless, look at him .... he's smart, handsome, polite, etc." She was about to continue....

"FUCK HIM!"

"Damn. Bae, my bad, I was just trying to help you..."

"Well, you ain't helping!" Greatness was thinking to himself, *"fuck this nigga, Demi. He's in the way anyway. I fuck with my Ville niggas, Read St. niggas. They're on the same type of time Segal St. gangs on."*

"Anyway, I'm still going to this meeting on Congress and West projects to see what's up, and what this soft bitch-ass got to say."

"I don't' need them niggas. Them niggas need me! They need Segal St."

What Demi G didn't know was that Greatness's crew had a street alliance with Read St., better known as "The Black Flag Gang."

"Yeah, I've been hearing about that Black Fang Gang. Y'all be robbing everything."

"Hell yeah! We just ran up in this spot in West Haven. We made off with $150,000, thanks to the help of the Candy Girls. We blessed them with $20,000 for their services. The other $130,000 we split up amongst the gang." Said Greatness.

"Yeah, you fucking right! They were acting like they weren't respecting this Black Flag shit."

"Listen, fuck all that......get my dick back hard. Spit on this shit, eat this dick up baby.... ummmm.... yeah, just like that......Yessssss, like that!"

"Damn Sade, you sucking this dick extra goooodddddd! I could see why Ghost love you so much .... With your nasty ass...."

"Whatever nigga! Whatever happen on Segal St. stays on Segal St.... FUCK JOEY GHOST!" Sade Said.

Chapter Eleven

The Meeting

6 p.m. the projects was lit with people. Cars were parked all around the projects. Some cars pulled-up in the first parking lot, and some pulled-up in the second parking lot on Bond St. Demi G parked his whip in the parking lot on West St., directly behind Uncle Joe's apartment. They were fifty-something deep. Demi G wasn't in any mood to be playing. He was furious about his spots being hit and he wanted answer.

"Look, I brought all of y'all here for two reasons. First reason, only my spots on the strip has been getting hit. Four times within the last 30 days, I need answers! Now!" Demi G said, with anger in his tone.

"My lil homie, TY-Ty said he heard one of the niggas, who robbed the spot say 'On the dead Villains', Y'all better not make one little move! So, this sounds like we could be dealing with Ville niggas, or the nigga swearing on the dead villains could just been said to throw us off." Demi G Said.

"Yeah, jack boys always try to throw niggas off by mentioning names of other niggas." Said Big Ether.

Big Ether is a local rapper from Congress and West. Son goes hard, and is soon to be signed. His career is looking promising. He got the Elm Buzzing on the map through his music.

"It's crazy cause these niggas ain't come, though the ninja spot trying no funny shit...." Said Big Ether. The ninja spot was the code name for Congress and West.

"We gotta tighten-up this period, because at this rate, we don't know who's next. At the end of the day, we are all Hill niggas, despite niggas having their own Movements and Cliques." Demi G said.

"That's a big fact!"

"4 times all day," Two niggas yelled out from the crowd. *"Hill niggas represent 4 times for the four letters in 'Hill'."*

Every hood in the Elm City rep a certain number. Some hoods have the same number, which doesn't necessarily mean that they're together, or have any type of alliances. When it boils down to how New Haven is, every hood is for itself.

"My second reason for calling this meeting is to let y'all know that any number y'all paying for coke I can top it.... Some may believe that I am trying to cut Joey Ghost neck, but Joey Ghost ain't from here! He's from the G."

The "G" is short for Ghetto, so everyone from the town just says "G" for short.

"He had his time, and a hell of a run; but now it's time for a change. My loyalty is to the Hill...... and the Hill alone." Said Demi G.

"Look at this snake-ass nigga! Want all the money, girls and power. Fuck boy, I don't give a fuck about NO HILL! It's Black Flags!" Greatness said to himself.

"So, everyone that's trying to see me gotta go through Ty-Ty." Said Demi G.

"So, what are we going to do about these stick-up kids?" Someone yelled from the crowd.

"Their day will come, but for now, we're not going to let anyone or anything interfere with this money." Said Demi G.

"This meeting is adjourned."

- - -

Agent Rose and Andrews sat in a gray Ford Crown Vic on Congress Ave., right in front of Bob's store.

"See, our informant was right about the meeting, look it's so many of them," said Rose.

"Yes, it is......but I don't see Dee Gotti, but there goes our star-informant jumping into his car. We'll know later when we debrief, he's going to have some juicy info." Said Andrews.

"Yes, we know for a fact that Dee Gotti is the head of this Hill gang, and he's also the leader of the C.A.B.'s; but there is never any sign of him. He's good, very good!" Said Agent Rose.

"We haven't seen his SL550 Benz lately either." Agent Andrews said, agreeing with his partner.

"We need to call and meet up with our star witness A.S.A.P. The Attorney-General is coming down on our asses, on getting some concrete evidence that will stick in court once we indict him."

"Dee Gotti is the man out here." Said Agent Rose.

"Hell yes, and our star-witness is going to provide us with the evidence we need, or if he decides not to cooperate with us...We're going to Arm-Career-Criminal him for that 357. Mag we caught on him." Said Agent Rose.

"That's a mandatory minimum of 15 years, plus he's a category (3), which would put him in the range of between 18 years to 21 years after accepting responsibility for his 3-point downward departure." Said Agent Andrews.

"The funny part about this situation is that he fell for the big lie they-all always fall for ... We can't even charge him with ACCA at all because he only has one drug prior." Said Agent Andrews, laughing hard.

"They always fall for what they don't know..."

"This fat, smelly, grimy, white bastard thinks this shit is funny!" Agent Rose thought to herself.

Chapter Twelve

GREATNESS

"What's up, cuz? How have you been on this side of town?" Said Greatness. Greatness was in the Ville on the corner of Read St. and Shelton Ave.

"Shit chilling, cuz. We still on tonight, right?" Said Olee.

"Yeah, Rickita said this one is only for $70,000, and I got to break her off $10,000, which is cool." Said Greatness.

"Shit! Whatever Black Flags with, I'm with. Just putting in work gets my dick hard!" Said Olee, with a devilish smirk on his face.

Rickita was driving up Shelton Ave. in her pink and white 2003 series BMW coup to meet up with them Black Flag nigga, so as to arrange the next lick.

Rickita turned right on Read St., and parked on the side of the corner store. She hopped out, ass-looking crazy. All the Black Flag Gangs eyes was stuck on stupid. She was definitely a bad bitch. Face-pretty as hell and body dumb-thick.

She walked towards Greatness, wearing a hot pick one-piece suit made by Gucci; She didn't have on any underwear, so her ass was bouncing everywhere.

"Hey Greatness, did you get my text?" Asked Rickita.

"Yeah, I got it, but didn't I tell yo ass not to ever text or call me? We communicate through Netta." Greatness said, trying to put on a show for his crew.

Rickita stood there for a brief second to catch herself from cursing Greatness the hell-out. Who in the hell does this boy thinks he's talking to? One phone call and I'll have his ass floating in a river somewhere! Rickita thought to herself, before cracking a smile, as if she didn't just hear Greatness' disrespectful ass.

"Yeah, I forgot.... But anyway, everything is set in motion." Rickita said.

"I'm with it, we just got to figure out how we going to get up out of Rockview. It's one way in and one way out." Said Greatness.

"We all know how these project niggas are giving it up. Most of the times, the police are scared to go up in that joint. So, we might have to shoot our way out." Said Greatness.

"Yeah, it definitely can get ugly." Said Rickita. *"They have about $70,000 in a safe, we gotta go get that! We don't let niggas flash money. They have to answer for that."*

"It's not about the money, Kita, it's about us being safe at the end of the day. You're not coming with us, so you don't

give a fuck about the Black Flag Gang. You only care about you getting your cut of the bread. This shit is dangerous, Kita." Said Greatness.

Rickita knew that everything Greatness was saying was valid, but she didn't give a flying fuck. She had bills that needed to be paid. She knew about the robbery that happened a few months back in West Haven, that left three dead. So as anything, shit could go south for the worse.

"You're right, I do want y'all to be safe bro, but Diamond said their niggas are extra hard from out there, especially the nigga she be tricking with." Said Rickita.

"Look, we going to figure this shit out the right way. Those projects ain't sweet. So, we're going to make a plan to get in and get out safe!" Greatness said.

"Okay, just give me a call bro. Let me know." Said Rickita. She wanted to ask about Demi G so badly, but every time she did, Greatness is quick to spazz on her. She was hoping Demi G was with him, so she could throw her shot.

"Damn, I can't never catch this nigga, Demi G... Maybe next time, I'll see his fine ass." Rickita thought to herself … She put a smile on her face, hopped in her pink Beemer and drove off.

"Yeah, that bitch is super thirsty, Olee." Said Greatness.

"Yeah, you gotta give it to her though. She's always been about her bread." Said Olee, while passing a blunt to Greatness.

"We need her tho. As long as she got her bitches sucking and fucking these sweet-ass niggas that are always running their mouths and flashing that bread, we gonna get this money." Said Greatness.

"On the dead Villains." Said Olee.

"So, we still on tonight?"

"I don't know bro, we gotta do more homework on these projects. I had hollered at Jan-Jan earlier. She's from the Manor from Rock view, but the only thing is Olee had cut greatness off before he could finish saying what Janjan told him."

"Oh, hell now! I know all about those woods. Them woods ain't right. Them niggas be having wild shootouts with each other in those woods." Said Olee.

Chapter Thirteen

Joey Ghost

Ghost was walking up Kensington St., in the Tre to meet up with his Tre niggas, so as to get his monthly payment.

"What's popping, Ghost?" Asked Trev.

"Ain't shit, just making my rounds. What's up with you, Trev?" Asked Ghost.

Trev handed him a brown paper bag of money.

"Shit, what's going on with that situation, with your young boy, Greatness?" Asked Trev.

"We're still working on that; he's been M.I.A. lately. He's always on point, we can't just run-up on him." Said Ghost.

"Shit, that nigga ain't hesitate to run-up and kill Black and Dawg, he ain't show no mercy, so why should we?" Trev said, looking right into the eyes of Ghost.

Ghost knew he had to do something about Greatness fast, or he was definitely going to lose his workers in the Tre, plus Tre's niggas had their suspicion about Ghost, having part in Black and Dawg getting smoked. They told Ghost if he didn't have anything to do with Black and Dawg, then he shouldn't have a problem with offing Greatness for his sins.

"Look Trev, we are on it right now, niggas got to give me some time to take care of Greatness. Greatness is running around with these young wild niggas from Read St., they call themselves Black Flag Gang. And not to mention all them Hill niggas just stopped fucking with me. I'm hearing my little nigga, Demi G, has got a whole new connect on me; That was the only time I would be close to Greatness, through Demi, and niggas barely see him." Trev was looking at Ghost like he had three heads. He had a gut feeling that Ghost was lying, and had his guys hit for them Hill niggas. He really wanted to shoot him right then and there, but he knew his own Tre niggas would be on his line. Especially them G-niggas.

"O.k., big bro, I'm just a phone call away, let me know. Myself and my K St. niggas are on deck, ready for war." Said Trev. "K" is short for Kensington St.

"I got eyes everywhere, lil bro, we just got to be smart about this. This nigga, Demi G, will know where to find Greatness. He's hard to find nowadays. He never calls me or tells me anything about his new connect. He just dropped-off what he owed, off to my runners, and that was the last time I heard from him." Said Ghost, as he was walking back to his Range Rover that was parked in front of this small complex that's in between Garden St. and Kensington St.

Ghost hopped into his truck, telling himself while driving off...... *"Damn! I gotta kill this nigga, Greatness, fast."*

- Demi G -

Demi G was running the whole Hill now. He got niggas from the other side fucking with him once he linked up with Wayne and Nino. Wayne and Nino had the Bridge on lock. The Bridge is a small section in the South. Instead of putting packs on Davenport Ave., he fronted weight to Ty-TY and had Ty-Ty put his own packs on Davenport Ave. to the rest of the posse...

"Damn, big cuz, we living the life." Said Ty-Ty, as Demi G drove down Congress Ave. in an all pearl-white 2003 745 BMW, with peanut butter interior. Everybody was outside. Normally, Congress Ave. was packed, but today, for some reason, the Ave. was extra lit. Everyone was waving as his Beemer floated up the Ave.

Demi G's waves were swimming, doing a 360. The Cuban link around his neck weighed about two kilograms.

"Yeah, this shit is on another level, kid." Said Demi G, referring to the bill he cleared that he owed Chuy.

Demi G took the 30 keys and added 9 ounces of cut to each key, and instead of making $24,000 he made 30,000. Demi G figured if he worked for no profit, he could get Chuy out of the way fast. He paid Chuyloco off in one month instead of five months. He gave Chuy $800,000, what he originally owed him for the 40 keys.

Then he gave him the $360,000 which left Demi G $40,000 to put in his pockets.

Chuy was so happy to see that Demi G was a true hustler. He was amazed that Demi G paid his homie's bill for those 18 kilos he lost. So, Chuy told Demi G, now he was going to charge him $18,000 per kilo and the new shipment is going to be 60 instead of 40. That will be 1.8 million he will see on his next flip. Demi G took a left on Bond St., then a left on Colombia Ave., before making the last left on West St. then hopped out.

"What's up, cuz?" Asked Killa Jay.

"I'm cool, cuz. What's the word out here?" Asked Demi G.

"It's kind of slow today, but it'll pick up around 3 p.m., rush hour time." Said Killa Jay.

"Yeah, I got that half of key for you right now anyway." Said Demi G.

Demi G signaled for Ty-Ty to get out of the car and hand Killa Jay the half of key.

"Hold up bro, I still got to give you $6,000 more from the last..." Said Killa Jay.

"So, you owe me $18,000 now, don't worry about it Killa. I got you kid." Said Demi G.

Ty-Ty took Killa Jay to the side of the project, which is called the Coov cut. They both walked out the Coov cut.

"Ayo cuz, what's up with your boy, Greatness? He's running around with Ville niggas from Read St. calling themselves Black Flag Gang. They don't even be on Stevens St. anymore. That shit is dead-over there." Said Killa Jay.

"Demi G knows all about that Black Flag Gang and is well aware of everything about Greatness and his Segal St. gang. Greatness does him and we are going to do us. Period!" Ty-Ty said, not wanting to show his real feelings about Greatness, because he knew no matter what Greatness was into, Demi G was never gonna let anyone harm his day-one friend. So, Ty-Ty just brushed him off with his quick answer.

Ring, ring, ring ...Demi G looked down at his phone and saw it was a call from Nue, so he quickly picked up.

"Hey baby. I miss you, and love you" Said Nue.

"Where you at, in the ninja spot?" Said Demi G.

*"*Yes. *You always in the dirty-ass Hill!"*

"Shut the fuck up. You know we get to that bag and we're the flyest." Said Demi G, Smiling to himself.

"Whatever nigga... but anyway, we gotta talk. I just got off the phone with Sade."

"O.K., where you at now?" Demi asked.

"I'm waiting on my flight to L.A., I'm at Bradley airport." Said Nue.

"So, I guess I'll see you in two days?"

"Copy.....Sounds like a plan." Said Demi G.

"Love you Boo Boo." Said Nue.

"Love you more sweetcakes." Said Demi G, laughing at the corny nicknames that they gave each other.

Demi jumped back in his 745.

"Ayo cuz, hit my jack when you got only a quarter left, then I will do the same thing."

"Next stop, we have to go see Dee Gotti in the Lover cut to give him his key." Said Demi G.

"Oh shit, Dee Gotti just hit my jack about an hour ago, and said cancel that because he's about to be out of town. I forgot to tell you that, big bro." said Ty-Ty.

"No Problem cuz. This Dee Gotti's third time doing that. Myself and him got to have a talk. That's bad business." Said Demi.

Chapter Fourteen

Joey Ghost

"I bet you $500 you won't hit that three-pointer again, Ghost." Said Ace G.

Joey Ghost was in his projects on Franklin St., shooting around on the basketball courts to release some stress. Ghost was stressing about losing the whole Hill which was his biggest profit.

"Naw... I'm good kid, it's too easy. I don't want to take your money." Said Joey Ghost.

Swish...... *"See how easy that was Ace? That would have been $500 gone that quick."* Joey Ghost was looking at Ace, smiling.

"What's on your mind, big homie? I can see it on your face." Said Ace G.

"Money." Said Ghost. "The streets ain't loyal no more. These little niggas have come across some real money, now they don't know how to act." Said Ghost.

"Big bro, you talking about Demi G?"

"Yeah, lil cuz. He got the whole Hill all fucked up right now. They calling him the King of the Hill." Said Ghost

"Yeah, I heard they came together and started calling themselves the H.B.O. and their response was, 'you already know!'" Said Ace. G.

"Yeah, I heard they came together and started calling themselves the H.B.O Movement. Hill Brothers Only. I was over there the other day at my aunt Mary Ann's crib when I heard a nigga yell out H.B.O. and their response was, 'you already know!'" Said Ace. G.

"That nigga, Demi G, is running a tight ship in the Hill. I'm talking about all the fiends in the Hill. They don't even want the work if it ain't from Demi G."

"Yeah, I know all about them H.B.O niggas. They took a lot of my profit in the Hill, but it ain't nothing tho." Said Ghost, before taking his last shot.

"Okay Ace…….. Let me know when you're ready to re-up. I'ma have Messy drop it off." Said Ghost, as he walks towards his black on black Range Rover that was sitting on all chrome 24-inch rims.

He hopped in his truck, looked in his rear-view mirror to make sure his cornrows were neat, edge up and mustache on point. He threw his Cartier's on his face and said to himself. *"Damn, I'm handsome."*

Ghost drove off slowly, looking around his project. Everyone was waving, "saying see you later", Ghost. Ghost was his hood's savior. Everyone loved and respected him.

Ghost took a left on Grand Ave., making his way to his big house in Bradford. He stopped at a red light and screamed out, "I

RUN THE FUCKING ELM CITY! AIN'T NO DAMN MEXICAN GOING TO RUN ME OUT OF MY CITY!"

- - -

- Black Flag -

"Ayo cuz, y'all ready?" Greatness asked his Black Flag Gang.

"Yeah cuz, we ready." Said Plizzy.

"Look, the homies on East Ramdell ready. Chirp them on the Nextel to see if they ready to make the hit."

Chirp, Chirp, Chirp…...Beep, Beep, Beep. "Yo cuz, we are at Valley St. now by the store, y'all ready?"

"Yeah…. we ready."

"Cuz, as soon as we hear the first shot, we going to hop out on East Ramdell, cause once y'all hit them on south Genesee, they gonna run in y'all direction." Said Olee.

"Copy." Replied Plizzy.

Greatness and the rest of the gang jumped out on the back side of South G, and knew that they were not going to be on point...

Blocka, Blocka, Blocka, Blocka. Plizzy was letting off his Glock 40.

Mocka, Mocka, Mocka.... Greatness let off his Beretta 9, catching a nigga right in the head. Three niggas were running through the backyards, on South G, towards East Ramdell.

"Oh shit! Flee, I think I'm hit." One of the 2-5 niggas said.

"Where at, homie?"

"In the leg..... ahh fuck!!"

"Just keep running.... try your best." Said Flee.

Blocka! Olee was on the side of the building, waiting. He shot Flee right in the back of the head.

G-Bo run down on the other two 2-5 niggas. Blocka, Blocka! "Black Flag stupid!" G-Bo had yelled, shooting them both in their heads.

"Damn cuz, you just smoke them niggas, and put them on top of each other! You still crazy as hell!" Said Olee.

"Fuck these niggas! They fucked that bag up, so we gotta make examples of niggas that fuck up Joey Ghost's money." Said G-Bo.

Chirp, Chirp......Beep, Beep.... *"Ayo, three niggas ran down towards y'all and we only heard three shots!"*

"That better have been three head-shots." Said Greatness.

"On the dead Villains. You know it, Cuz! Black Flag Gang." Said Olee.

Chapter Fifteen

Demi G

Demi G was driving on Route 34, on his way to a small town called Oxford. He pulled up to the biggest house on this quiet street. He's seen a 2003 G63 Benz G-Wagon parked right in front of the 4-door garage.

"H.B.O." Dee Gotti said, as he watched Demi G get out of his whip.

"You already know." Responded Demi G.

"Damn cuz, you out here, laying low in the cut." Said Demi G.

"Shit! You ought not to be here, bro; this shit out here is hectic. I wanted to holla at you about a few things."

"Okay, talk to me my G". said Demi G.

"Lately, I've been followed by some type of law enforcement. I been seeing this gray Crowd Vic everywhere I go." Said Dee Gotti.

"So, that's why you keep changing your number?" Asked Demi G.

"Damn right, cuz." Said Gotti. *"I feel we got an informant in the hood. Someone that's close to me. So, with that*

being said cuz, I'm out the game for a little time, homie. I got Douggie from the lover cut, going to replace me."

Demi G just stood there, speechless; shaking his head. He couldn't believe what he was hearing.

"Not Congress' finest." Said Demi G.

"Yeah, you heard right, lil cuz. I got everything I need, plus more out of the game. Douggie is my lil cuz. You can trust him. He's official. But anyway, Demi, why did I hear you dropped out of Yale and quit your internship?" Gotti asked, with a sign of disappointment on his face.

"I had to drop out, bro. It's a long story, but I'll be back at it soon. Right now, I have too much on my plate to fully focus on school. I'm not going to half-step it." Said Demi G.

"Yeah cuz, you are super smart. Don't waste it on these streets. The Elm city is a love-hate city. You're either going to love it or hate it. And the game we play sooner or later; we're going to hate this shit. So, when you get your affairs in order lil bro, get back in school and change this world we're living in." Said Dee Gotti.

Demi G had always looked up to Dee Gotti, and when he was a little nigga, he wanted to be a part of the Congress Ave Brothers; but Demi decided to fuck with dark-skinned Jack and get down with Davenport posse. Even though Demi G lived on Stevens st. right off Davenport Ave., it was still considered Davenport Ave.

"Cuz, I salute you for your decision. If you ever decide to change your mind, you know where I'm at. 4 times cuz, H.B.O," said Demi G.

"You already Know!" Responded Dee Gotti.

- - -

- Ty-Ty -

"Nigga......it's a 250 an hour, not 150." Said Evelyn.

"Bitch, that's all I'm giving you! Your pussy was trash; you don't even have any walls. The Candy Girls never sent me a trash bitch! I don't know why Rickita sent you anyway." Said Ty-Ty.

"Nah, we got a surprise for you." Said Evelyn.

"A surprise? Shit, I hope it's free cause I had to beat my dick to bust a nut. With your garbage-ass-pussy." Ty-Ty said, while he laughed.

"You should be somewhere on the street selling that pussy. I can't wait to call and tell Rickita about this one." Said Ty-Ty.

As Ty-Ty was getting dressed, putting on his jeans, Evelyn sent a text to one of the Black-Flag-Gang members saying, *"I got him, come on now!"*

Ty-Ty was fixing his clothes and got mad for being late to drop-off the half-a-bird on Ward St. to Bear back. Damn! Ty-Ty thought to himself. *"I know Bear going to be upset. But I had to get my dick wet."*

On the side of the hoe house on Elliot St., Lunatic and Plizzy tied their black bandana around their faces. They crept down through the hallway. Evelyn snuck out the room and looked at the two masked up, pointing in the direction of the room Ty-Ty was in ... Blocka!

Ty-Ty didn't see it coming. He was shot right on the side of his head, right about his temple. Brains flew everywhere. Lunatic was in shock as he saw Ty-Ty brains scattered all over the room.

"Ayo cuz, call Greatness and let him know the job is done." Said Plizzy.

Chapter Sixteen

Sade

"Hey Boo Boo. Where you at?" Asked Sade.

Greatness was happy as hell Sade finally called him. He has been waiting on her to duck Ghost, so he could feel that wet, tight pussy again.

"Shit, leaving Read St. right now, bout to ride out Fair Haven." Said Greatness.

"Where you at tho?"

"Nigga, you know where I'm at. Trying to get rid of this old nigga and come get some of that young dick." Said Sade.

"Is that right!" Greatness said, rubbing his manhood through his jeans. *"I can't wait to pound that fat pussy."*

"Okay, go get a room at the super 8 in West Haven."

"Sade meet me there around 7p.m."

Sade smiled to herself, knowing that she had the young vicious nigga right where she wanted him. Now, she could continue to gather all the information she needs from him. Greatness ran his mouth worse than a bitch in high school.

Sade looked over to Joey Ghost. "Baby, this is too easy! You gotta put me on a harder task." Sade said, while smiling.

"Nah baby......I need you to fuck him good, and keep fucking him. Sade, keep him coming back for more."

Ghost was thinking to himself about how important it is to keep Greatness close, because he knew Greatness was vicious, unpredictable, and answered to no one, but maybe Demi G.

"Yeah, I know......and that's the crazy part. Demi G is the boss around there now, so if anyone would have the Feds watching them, it would be Demi G, not Dee Gotti." Said Ghost.

"Yeah babe, that's a fact. This shit ain't making any sense." Said Sade.

"Look baby, make sure you get any info you can from Greatness about this situation. This shit could somehow lead back to us. The name, Lonnie Jones, don't sound familiar to me."

Lonnie Jones is the name of the Federal Informant given to Ghost by the dirty cop he got on his payroll.

"So, mention the informant's name to Greatness after y'all pop that E-pill. He'll be running his mouth like no other." Said Ghost.

"Now, get your sexy ass over here. Daddy has been dying to taste your juices. I'm thirsty!" Said Ghost.

"Babeee.......... Stopppp! You're so nasty." Sade said, as she slid her panties down.

"You love this nasty shit." Said Ghost, licking his lips, ready to eat Sade's ass.

Sade got in the doggy style position and threw her ass in the air. *"Go ahead baby, grab those cheeks and spread that shit!"* Said Ghost as he spat on Sade's asshole, sucking like his life depended on it.

"Ahhhhh......Yessss, Daddy......just ......Like......that!" Sade moaned out.

Chapter Seventeen

Demi G was in Bridgeport, at seaside park driving around the loop really slow. He just got finished dropping off 2 kilos to one of his guys from Greens projects in Bridgeport.

Demi G was looking like a real boss in his pearl white 7451 BMW. All the honeys was sweating him looking in his window, wondering who the hell he was because they never seen the young boss before. Demi G wasn't worrying about no females, his only concern at the time was money.

Demi G was leaving the park about to hop on I-95 North, heading to the Elm when his phone rung…..

"Yo, what's cracking, cuz?" Said Demi G.

"Man……this is bad! Cuz this is really bad!" Said Jo-Jo.

"What the fuck you talking about Jo-Jo? Speak!" Said Demi G, yelling through the phone.

"Man, they found Ty-Ty dead on the corner of Day St. and George St. right in front of the store in the Tre." Said Jo-Jo.

"What? ……….How? Noooooo!" Demi G said, crying.

Demi G immediately hopped back on the highway, flying back to town.

"Hey cuz, shit real! Them Tre niggas had to have killed him. They shot my boy in his head!" Jo-Jo added.

"Why would Ty-Ty be in the Tre in the first place? He told me he was on his way to serve Bear Back on Ward St., that was the last time I spoke to him." Said Demi G.

Tears started flowing rapidly from Demi G's eyes, thinking how he was going to look in the face of Ty-Ty's mother and tell her that her son is gone. She knows I was supposed to be the one to protect him and shield him from the streets.

"Damn, I let my little man down! That was my nigga, I brought him off the porch and introduced him to the D.P.P. family. Now he's dead." Said Demi G.

"Where is his car?" Asked Demi G.

"No one knows bro." said Jo-Jo.

"They said he was Dead on arrival! He was already dead when they found him, Demi!"

"This shit isn't adding up right now at all, Jo-Jo. Look, do me a favor, go over there where they found Ty-Ty and see if anyone heard any shots in the area."

"Copy big cuz, I'm on it." Said Jo-Jo.

"And send a few niggas over to Day St. projects and fire that shit down until further notice. Until we figure out who's behind little cuz getting smoked." Said Demi G.

"Say no more big cuz." Jo-Jo did as he was told after hanging up the phone.

Demi G was doing about 120 miles per hour in deep thought, thinking about his little man, until he received another phone call.

"Yo, yo, yo…….Cuz someone just ran up in your mom's crib about 10 minutes ago! Them niggas had on all-black and they kidnapped your mom." Said Smoke.

"Wha…..Wha….What you just say?" Demi G asked, thinking his ears were playing tricks on him.

"Yo, someone just kidnapped your mother, I said!" Smoke said, repeating himself.

"Noooooo!" Demi G hung up. Picking up more speed. He was scared for his mom's life.

- - -

- Summertime of 1994 -

Demi always visited his aunt, Lanisha. She lived in Franklin St. projects, The Ghetto…....A.K.A….The G.

Demi went outside to play with the rest of the kids in the projects, as any 10-year-old kid would do. As Demi walked to the middle of the projects, he just stood, looking around. He saw so many kids running around playing, enjoying themselves. It was a big difference coming from the inner city in the Hill to seeing how it was in the projects. Stevens St. only had a block party once a year, but the projects seemed like every day was a block party....

"Ayo......You......Where you from?" Trice yelled out from her back porch.

Demi looked around to see who was talking to him. He saw a really pretty girl looking at him, smiling.

"Yeah you.... Where you from? Cause you ain't from around here." Said the little pretty girl.

"The Hill.... I'm from the Hill." Said Demi.

"Where?" Trice asked again, as if she didn't just hear Demi say the Hill.

"The Hill." Demi yelled louder.

Everything in the center of the projects just stopped. Everything just went quiet once everyone heard the word Hill. If you were not from the Tre, Tribe, or Eastern Circle, you had no business in G.

Demi grew nervous once he noticed all the kids staring at him. All the old people were looking out their windows. The basketball stopped bouncing, the little girls stopped double-ditching, and the dice stopped rolling.

It actually looked like the world just had paused and stood at a standstill, until Demi saw four boys with all their fists balled-up, walking in his direction. Demi didn't run, he stood right there.... Pow! Someone sucker-punched Demi right in the back of the head.

Demi dropped to the pavement and immediately got back up, swinging all crazy. 5 boys were jumping Demi, punching him all in the face, but Demi wasn't backing down. He was steady, swinging back, taking his ass whooping.

"Get the fuck off him now!" Said an older dude that was from the G. All the young boys did as they were told and stopped jumping Demi. Demi had two swollen eyes, knots on his head, and a busted lip. Right before the older guy had ordered them to get off him, Demi fell to the ground.

"Get up kid." The older guy said. *"How old are you?"*

"I'm 10 years old." Said Demi G.

The older guy looked towards the young boys that had just jumped Demi and said *"Y'all should be ashamed of yourselves. Y'all about 14 or 15 years old, this little nigga is only 10 years old, and y'all couldn't clean him up."* Ghost said, shaking his head.

"What's your name?" Ghost asked Demi.

"Demi." Demi responded.

118

"Demi? Where you from Demi?"

Demi looked at the boys that just jumped him breathing heavily, and ready for more and said ......I'm from the Hill.

"Oohhhh, that's why they jumped you." The older guy said.

"My name is Joey Ghost. I'm from these projects......As a matter of fact, I run these projects. Look kid, these kids fight all the time out here. The reason why I stopped the fight was because I saw some heart in you. And you didn't look familiar. You didn't run or back down. Instead, you ran straight towards the smoke." Said Joey Gost.

"Look kid, come on and let me take you home. You gotta clean yourself up. Who are you out here with?" Asked Joey Ghost.

"My aunt, Lanisha." Said Demi G.

"Nisha's your aunt?"

"Yeah, that's my mother's sister." Said Demi G.

"Me and Nisha go way back. I'ma page her on her beeper, and let her know I'm taking you home." Said Ghost.

"Where you live at in the Hill?"

"Stevens St., right off Davenport Ave." said Demi G.

"O.k., I got some guys over there……(S.S.P.) Stevens St. Posse." Said Ghost.

"Listen little nigga, you got heart and you seem like you are intelligent ……Right?" Said Ghost.

"Look, we're going to call you Demi-God because you're in my neighborhood, I'm GOD!" Joey Ghost said, laughing.

"So, your name is Demi G, my little guy." They walked to Franklin St. and hopped in Ghost's 95 Lexus 400 Gs parked in the lot. Ghost just looked at Demi G and told him, "Lil cuz, you gonna be a problem when you get older."

Joey Ghost drove his black-on-black Lexus through downtown. He had 20-inch rim shining on his ship with no tints, straight fish bowling.

Joey Ghost entered into the Hill on Congress Ave. He thought to himself about all the bread that he could get in the Hill. Ghost looked down at Demi G and said, "You only 10 years old, right?"

"Yes Sir." Demi G replied.

"Well, in about 3 or maybe 4 years, I'm going to make you a boss around here." Said Ghost.

"Look here, lil cuz, take my beeper number. Anything you need make sure you don't hesitate to let me know. Sneakers, food, clothes, and whatever else you may need." Said Ghost.

"And whenever you come back to the G, let me know first. You got a lifetime Ghetto pass."

Demi G was confused as to why Ghost liked him so much, and what the hell was a ghetto pass? Well, he figured whatever it was, it had to be a good thing.

"O.k. Sir, thank you." Said Demi G.

"Look, don't call me sir, call me O.G. or Joey Ghost from here on out." Said Ghost.

"O.k. sir, I mean O.G." said Demi G, smiling.

Ghost took a right down Kossuth St. then left on Davenport Ave. and made another right on Stevens St.

"Look, lil cuz, I meant what was said from here on out. We got a bond. You make sure you hit me on my hip." Said Ghost.

"O.k., O.G.... I got you." Said Demi G.

Joey Ghost went in his pocket and pulled out $200 in 20's and gave it to Demi G.

Demi G was happy as hell, he's never seen money like that before. He had a big smile on his face.

"Thank you O.G. Thank you!" Said Demi G again.

"Every time you get all A's on your report card in school, I'ma give you $500 plus the new Jordans, O.k. Demi?

Now get out and always remember to save your money and don't spend it all in one place."

"*O.k. O.G"* said Demi G. Demi got out of the car and stared at Ghost as he drove off and said, *"He really is GOD."*

Chapter Eighteen

Rickita

Rickita was sitting on her porch in deep thought about a conversation she just had with her father over the phone. She was contemplating her next big move.

Rickita was riding in a new four door pink Audi A6, another addition to her pink car collection. She was driving down Route 34 going towards the Elm City. She was heading to pick up her hooker, Evelyn. As she entered the Hill on Elliot St., Evelyn was standing right in front, looking so sexy and adorable. She could pull a nigga on her worst day.

"Hey bitch."

"Hey Kita baby." Said Evelyn, as she jogged off the porch, getting in the passenger side of the A6. "Where are we going, bitch?"

"Shit, just cruising the Elm, it's a slow day anyway, so there's no need to be sitting and waiting on tricks."

Rickita was driving down Sylvan Ave.; she took a right on Howard Ave. then a left on York St. right on the side of Yale New Heaven Hospital.

Rickita pulled up to the red light, waiting to take that right on Richard Lee Highway I-91.

Evelyn started to get really nervous because she never seen Rickita so quiet. Rickita wasn't saying a word.

"Hey bitch, where we going?" Asked Evelyn.

"I told you we're just driving around." Said Kita.

"O.K., but usually we just drive around in town, where everybody is at. We don't never drive out of the city," said Evelyn.

The light turned green and Kita took the right hopping on I-91 North without saying a word back to Evelyn. She drove until she reached exit 8, jumping off the highway onto Middleton Ave. She then took a right on a little small street and parked. Rickita told Evelyn to get out of the car. Evelyn was scared shitless.

"For what? What we doing out here?" Evelyn asked, looking around to see no one.

"Bitch, get the fuck out the car! I'm not going to tell you again." Yelled Kita. Evelyn did as she was told, scared for her life. Rickita pulled out her 380. Ruger.

"Sorry, sorry Kita, needed the money." Evelyn cried, pleading her case.

"Bitch, why the fuck was you a part of that hit? When the Candy Girls had nothing to do with it?" Said Rickita.

"I needed the money. Five thousand to help kill Ty-Ty."

"And you had the nerve to do that shit to my hoe's house. Dumb-Ass Bitch!" Yelled Kita.

"I'm sorry, I won't do it again, I promise." Evelyn said, crying.

"Bitch, there won't be an again!" Blocka! Rickita shot Evelyn in her head, killing her instantly.

Rickita was furious at Greatness and the Black Flag Gang. She knew that she had to put an end to their relationship. The Black Flag Gang was becoming too reckless for the Candy Girls. Their names were in everything but a casket.

Rickita didn't want the Candy Girls to associate with nothing that had to do with Greatness and his crew. Rickita and her crew's name were starting to ring bells for siding the Black Flag Gang in some of their sling.

Yeah, the Candy Girls caught a couple of licks with them, but all those personal licks, Rickita had no parts in it. Rickita got on her phone, *"Hey Daddy, it's done."* Confirming that Evelyn was gone.

- - -

- Kidnapping-

It was one of those beautiful hot summer days. Mrs. Edwards was sitting on her porch on Stevens St. watching all the kids run up and down the street. She thought to herself how Stevens St. been quiet lately with illegal activity, but from time-to-time, she would hear gunshots in the neighborhood.

"Hey Ms. Edwards. How you doing today?" Asked Mary. Mary was walking up the street coming from the store on Davenport and Stevens St.

"I'm doing fine sweetheart, thank you for asking." Said Ms. Edwards.

Ms. Edwards saw Mary walking to the store on a few different occasions, while sitting in her chair, looking through the window. But today, the look on Mary's face was weird. She noticed Mary staring extra hard at her house. Mary made her way up the street towards Sylvan Ave.

Ms. Edwards was an original (S.S.P.) member back in the early 80's. S.S.P. They were known for their dime bags of crack. The biggest, cheapest, and purest cocaine in the city. So, you know she's seen a lot of paper back in her day. And you know the saying. *"More money, more problem."* Ms. Edwards could sense when something wasn't right.

Ms. Edwards cocked her glock back, making sure she had a bullet in the head. She didn't want to tell her son that she's seen Mary with Greatness a few months back, coming out of Greatness's mother's house. She knew that her son was in love with a lying little whore. When it came to Mary, she couldn't do any wrong in Demi G's eyes.

Ms. Edwards didn't want to see Demi G's heart broke, so she kept it a secret. Plus, she wanted her baby to focus on college and getting out of the mean streets of the Elm City. Ms. Edwards placed her Glock under her pillow, before she took her daily nap, as she dozed off to sleep, she felt a cold barrel touch the middle of her forehead.

"Bitch if you even think about moving towards grabbing that gun underneath your pillow, I'ma blow your fucking face off." Said Nasty.

Ms. Edwards was so scared and disappointed in herself for letting down her guard. Nasty duck taped her mouth, Lunatic grabbed her legs, and Olee helped to make sure everything went smooth.

"Bitch, you worth about a half-a-mill right now." Said Nasty.

"Yeah, we definitely need it too. Word to D-Lover!"

"We need this check. Your son is gonna cough this $500,000."

When Ms. Edwards heard, *"Word to D-Lover"* she knew that these was the dumb kids from the neighborhood. When they threw Ms. Edwards in the back seat of the car, she heard Mary's voice say, *"Damn! We finally got this old bitch. Where we at with her?"* Asked Mary.

"Up top in the Ville on Suffield."

- - -

- Ghost...1996 -

Joey Ghost was driving in his brand new Acura Legend on his way to pick up Demi G on Steven St.

"What's up cuz?"

"I'm cooling." Said Demi G.

"Come on, hop in, I'm taking you shopping today, lil cuz. We about to go to New York City and shop all-up and down Fordham in the Bronx."

Demi G was unfamiliar with the Bronx, but if Joey Ghost was taking him shopping it was all good with him.

"Damn, lil cuz! Straight A's and the honor roll? I can't believe how smart you are." Said Joey Ghost, as he hopped on I-95 South going towards New York.

"So, what else is going on with you besides school?" Asked Ghost.

"Nothing really O.G......I really like this girl named Jessica, but she dissed me for this fat dirty-ass nigga! And I told her that!" Said Demi G, laughing a little.

"You told her what?" Asked Ghost.

"I told her...."

"Listen, don't ever do that again." Ghost told Demi G.

"Do what again?" Asked Demi.

"Tell a female that a nigga she's attracted to is fat and dirty. That's some hating shit!" Ghost schooled Demi G.

"Don't ever talk bad about a nigga to any females at all. Because what a female sees in a man you can never understand. You're not gay, right?"

"Hell Nah." Demi G quickly responded.

"That's my point! So, who are you to determine what she sees or like in another guy? It will only make it look like your intentions are to make her look at dudes in the same way you look at them. Which is impossible, because she's a female and you're a male."

"See, females get a pass to talk shit about other females to niggas, because it's just a part of their nature. Us niggas tho,

aren't supposed to engage in any form of gossip to a female about another man. Now, what happens if she goes back and repeats to him what you said?" Ghost asked Demi G, making all the sense.

"I never looked at it like that." Said Demi G.

"The nigga is going to feel like you're hating on him and might want to bust your shit!' Said Ghost.

Demi G was just sitting there, listening to his O.G. sucking up all the game.

"Now y'all beefing over some pussy! God forbid if any of y'all get locked up... She ain't gonna be around. She ain't gonna write you; oh, she's damn sure ain't coming to no visiting room. She will have a whole new nigga before you even get sentenced." Said Ghost.

"So, I don't ever want to hear you talk bad about a nigga to a female again! You got it?" Ghost asked.

"Yeah, I got you." Said Demi G.

"We'll leave that for them bitch-ass niggas, because that's what bitches do!" Said Ghost.

Ghost was instilling morals, principles and honor which eventually equal-out to gaining respect. Every time Ghost got with Demi G, he schooled him on how shiesty the game was.

Joey Ghost was cruising up I-95 South just passing Stamford, Ct.

"I don't want to keep bringing this back up O.G. but I got to." Said Demi G.

"Talk." Said Ghost.

"So, what should I do if the girl doesn't like me then, is it fuck her?"

"Demi G, she will regret it one day." Said Ghost. *"Look, in the game of life there will always be another nigga shining more than you. There's always going to be somebody below you and higher than you. The niggas that's shining more than you, you gotta learn from them and learn from their mistakes. Do not try to outshine them because then you will look stupid. When you get out of school, some of them same niggas, you going to say, "Damn homie, back in High school, you was the man homie, what the fuck happened to you?" Take your time. Your shine is coming. No need to rush, Demi G. I'm going to make sure of that. It's a bunch of losers out there."*

"But I'll be damned if you're going to turn out to be one of those losers. You're going to be a different type of nigga. I'ma teach you how to be a real nigga that stands on principles." Joey Ghost just hopped off on exit 5 about to make a right on Jerome Ave. heading towards Fordham Fd.

"Look kid, you point and I'll buy." Said Ghost.

131

"*O.k., O.G.*" said Demi G, with the biggest cool-ass smile on his face.

"*I got you kid, whatever you want.*" Said Joey Ghost.

- - -

- Lunatic -

"*Yo cuz, that's a good look. We're about to get paid.*" Lunatic was saying to Mary, as she was dropping him off on Greenwood and Sylvan.

"*Yeah, this one was kind of an easy one. It only took us about a week to snatch her old ass and that soft-ass nigga gonna bring us half a mil A.S.A.P.,*" said Mary.

"*Yeah, that soft-ass nigga that used to be your man! HA HA HA...*" Lunatic laughed.

"*Yeah, right... that was never my man. He thought we were together and he never saw this pussy. This pussy is Greatness' and always has been.*" Mary said, laughing, showing her pretty white teeth. Mary pulled up on Sylvan Ave. As Lunatic was getting out of the car he said, "*Black Flag.*"

"*Money Bag!*" Mary said, as she sped off.

Lunatic was walking to his crib on Sylvan Ave. until he heard someone call out his government name in a low voice. "*Lonnie.........Lonnie.*" He heard it again.

Lunatic pulled out his 9mm Roger as he continued walking towards Greenwood St.

Greenwood St. is a very dark street, due to the shadows from the big building that's on Sylvan Ave. Even the street lights aren't enough to help light up Greenwood St., Lunatic walked towards the corner until he saw a figure that looked too familiar.

"Oh shit.........O.G. what's up, nigga?" Lunatic said, as he went to put his gun away.

"What's up Lonnie?" Ghost asked.

"Shit... I'm cooling, cuz." Lunatic said, while wondering if he was in trouble with Ghost over all those personal hits he's been doing off the books... or did Ghost find out about Demi's mother's kidnapping?

"I know you're wondering why I'm calling you by your government name. Lonnie Jones.... Huh?" Said Ghost.

"I don't know why, honestly." Lunatic said, showing signs that he was nervous.

"Because that's what them people you work for call you!"

"Whaaat people?" Said Lunatic.

"The fucking Feds! Because you're a fucking RAT!" Ghost yelled at him before pulling out his Python 357. Magnum.

He placed the long barrel of the gun to the right of Lunatic's head.

"Now.... That ain't true, O.G. I've never told on anyone I fuck with......" Lunatic said, as he was crying, scared for his life.

"Yes...Ooooo yes, you have! Lonnie, you're ratting on Dee Gotti!" Said Ghost.

"But......But Ghost, we don't fuck with him anyway. Fuck Dee Gotti! They were trying to give me 20 years for a gun O.G... So, I lied and put the Feds on him. I did that to save us, Ghost. The Feds were interested in you at first, until I pointed them in Dee Gotti's direction." Said Lunatic.

"So, let me get this right ... You figure that just because you didn't rat on someone in your inner circle, that it would make it o.k?" Said Ghost.

"Yeah ......I mean we don't fuck with them Congress Ave. boys anyway. Please, don't shoot me, I never mentioned anyone's name in the team. Listen...Please.........Don't" Lunatic said, pleading for his life.

"Listen, Oooo Lonnie boy......If you gave any information to the law, whether you were lying or not .... You corroborated. That makes you a fucking RAT! And all rats are to be exterminated." Said Ghost.

Ghost looked back at his Range Rover and waved. All that was seen was a short-stocky nigga with two twin Glocks, approaching him with them, aimed at his melon.

Ghost walked back and got in his truck.

Blocka, Blocka, Blocka, Blocka!

"See, I ain't never ever liked none of you Hill niggas, anyway. I'm a true G nigga to the core! Project baby! I always wanted to catch me a Black Flag nigga!"

"Ayo, why every time you kill someone, you gotta sit there with them and make a speech?" Ghost yelled at Messy.

"That's what I do, O. G.........Talk to the dead." Messy said, as he looked at the four holes in Lunatic's face.

"Now you got four holes in your face! You dead-repping the Hill four times all day now." Said Messy.

Messy started walking slowly towards the Range Rover. Ghost just shook his head thinking to himself, *"This little motherfucker is crazy, but he's a real killer."*

"I rather have him on my side than have him going against me ..." Ghost thought to himself.

135

Chapter Nineteen

Rickita

On the back road heading to Waterbury from the Elm City, Rickita was on her way to see one of her best clients. Whenever the name "Big$$$" came across her caller I.D., She knew that she was going to make nothing less than $10,000. Her client always requested two of her thickest hoes, Chocolate and Vanilla.

Chocolate was obviously dark-skinned. 5'5, hazel eyes, with the fattest ass and no stomach. Vanilla on the other hand was a light-skinned version of Megan Good, but just a little taller. Her face was her money-maker, she had flawless beauty. Standing at 5'10 with hips out of this world. Vanilla was definitely a baddie!

Rickita parked on South Main St. in Waterbury, at the exact same spot that she would pull-up to every other week.

Rickita wished she didn't have to always attend her client's session with chocolate and Vanilla, but her client wanted Rickita to sit in and watch him have sex with them.

He knew he couldn't have her join in, so having her watch him was his next best option. Rickita never actually really sold her own pussy. She just used her own sex appeal to pull new clients, making them believe she does. And before they knew it, she had all of their money.

"This money is good." Said Vanilla. *"But his dick is so small!"*

"Y'all hoes need to shut the fuck up! This little-dick nigga is paying $10,000 for two hours and all y'all thinking about is busting a nut?" Said Rickita, shaking her head.

"Bitch ... We're the Candy Girls. We about a buck, not a nut!" The three Candy Girls got out of the pink Audi A6 and walked in the building to meet up with their trick.

"Hey my friends ... Y'all are a little late getting here. I should deduct from y'all pay." Said Chuyloco.

"Yeah, right nigga! We are only about 5 minutes late and you're talking about deducting someone's pay... Nigga please!" Rickita said, in a smart tone.

"Nah.... I'm just playing mommy, Damn Kita, ease up a little baby." Said Chuyloco.

Chuyloco entered his master bedroom with his arms around both hoes. Chuy got on the bed with both Chocolate and Vanilla on each side of him. Rickita sat right in front of them.

Chocolate took his dick from up under his Vantage Armani robe and started sucking. Vanilla made her way to Chuy's balls, putting both balls in her mouth at the same time. "Damn this nigga got some big ass balls with a little-ass dick!" Vanilla thought to herself, as she sucked away.

"Y'all bitches get that money!" Yelled Rickita.

Rickita was sitting in a chair, looking so sexy with her fat, soft ass hanging off the sides of the chair.

Chuy was laying there watching Rickita the whole time.

"Ahhh......Shit....... Damn......This feels so good and you're so beautiful Kita. I wish you could join us. I will pay another $10,000 just for you to join." Said Chuyloco.

"Nah......Nigga! That will never happen." Said Rickita.

"Damn! It was worth a try!" Chuyloco was always offering extra money to fuck Rickita, but Rickita would never allow that happen, no matter what the price was.

After about two hours of fucking and sucking, Chuy was exhausted. He always enjoyed himself when he had his sessions with the Candy Girls.

Chocolate and Vanilla got dressed and went and sat in the Audi, while Rickita and Chuy chatted.

"So, Kita ... What's up with your boy, Demi G?" Asked Chuyloco.

"Shit! ... You would know better than me. You're the one that supplies him." Said Rickita.

"I don't supply anyone personally. I see him once in a while. I'm hearing great things about him. But I'm also hearing

through the grapevine that he's having dispute with the Black Flag Gang, and any disputes are always bad for business." Said Chuyloco.

"Demi G has been bringing in a lot of money. I feel like these issues with Demi G and Black Flag Gang are going to cut into my business."

"That's a fact." Said Kita.

Rickita was the one who informed Chuy on who Demi G is, and who he was tied to, when Chuy first met Demi G downtown. Rickita knew all about the beef between Joey Ghost and Chuy's cartel that has been going on since the 80's.

So, when Chuy learned through Rickita about Demi G, and his association with Ghost; he got extra excited and knew he had to recruit him. Chuyloco didn't have any knowledge of the relationship between Rickita and Joey Ghost; and Rickita had every intention of keeping Chuy in the dark about it.

Shit, she figured that this nigga was bringing her in $20,000 a month, so she was willing to keep this a secret forever. After they talked about 15 more minutes, Rickita was ready to move on to collect her next check.

"O.k. Chuy.... So, I will see you in two weeks, right?" Said Rickita.

"Yes......As long as you come and see me with them. I'll be seeing you every two weeks." Chuyloco said, smiling.

Rickita stood up and put on her pink-leather Gucci jacket, and she walked out of the building and jumped in her car.

"Y'all bitches need to go get in the shower. Y'all smell like sweaty ass and Mexican balls!" She said, as she drove off heading back to the New Haven on the back roads.

Chapter Twenty

1996

"Aunty Nene." Said Demi, calling his aunt by the nicknames that her family gave her. Demi was busy playing away on his Super Nintendo.

"Boy.... What the hell do you want? Every ten minutes you calling my damn name!" Said Lanisha.

"Can you make me some baked ziti? Please.." Asked Demi.

"Boy, go and brush your teeth. It's 7 in the morning and you talking about some damn ziti......Nigga please." Lanisha said.

"Well, then later please?" Demi begged his aunt.

"I will think about it, boy....... Now, leave me the hell alone and stop yelling my name." Said Lanisha. *"Why don't you go outside or something with your friends, Larry and T-Nice. They're the only ones that really like you out here in these projects."* Said Lanisha

Little did Lanisha know her nephew and his two friends Larry Love and T-Nice worked the 12 to 4 p.m. shift on Hamilton side. When Demi G came outside, he saw a lot of niggas in the projects that didn't like him because he was from the Hill. But due to him being under the wing of Ghost, no one would dare lay a finger on him. The most they would do is talk shit behind his back.

"Ayo... What's up, cuz?" Said Larry Love. They were standing on the Hamilton side.

"You got the next pack? T-Nice just took off to get Yummy in the back of the projects." Said Larry Love.

"Ooooo, Okay. What's up with you tho?" Said Demi. Demi was fresh to death in his Air Jordan sweat-suit and Retro 9 Jays. He had a big Cuban Link Chain around his neck.

As he walked around back of the building, he saw Trice. Since the first time he laid eyes on her, he had real crush on Trice. She was there a couple years ago when he got jumped. She thought he was so brave for not running and standing his ground.

"How you doing, Trice?" Said Demi G.

"I'm good, Demi, are you okay?"

"Yeah, I'm cool."

Trice was standing there stuck looking into Demi's eyes, trying her best not to blush, but it wasn't working. Her face was as red as a strawberry.

Trice thought Demi G was so handsome, but she had a boyfriend, which was this crazy little nigga named Messy, who had the whole projects scared of him.

Joey Ghost pulled up in his Acura Legend and parked. Messy jumped out the passenger side of the whip. Messy was really short. About 5'2 and light-skinned, with curly hair. He walked towards Demi G and Trice.

"Here little nigga ... And don't fuck this pack up!"
Messy told Demi. Messy and Demi G was actually the same age. Messy never really liked Demi G, so whenever he could throw a jab and try to belittle him, he did.

Demi G felt Messy was only trying to play him because Trice was present. Messy grabbed Trice by the arm and told her, *"Didn't I tell you to stop talking to this Hill nigga?"*

"He's harmless, Messy! He hangs in the projects with us." Said Trice.

"But, you got all the other Ghetto boys to talk to, but yet, I always catch you in that nigga's face." Said Messy, with jealousy written all over his face.

Without saying a word, Trice rolled her eyes and turned to walk away. She went back to the Franklin St. side of the projects. Demi walked up to Joey Ghost.

"What's up, O.G.?" Said Demi.

"How you doing out here, kid?" Said Ghost.

"I Just got out here, I love this car, O.G.," said Demi

"When you turn 16 and get your license, it's yours. As long as you stay in school and keep up the good grades, you can have it." Said Ghost. Demi just stood there smiling.

"Did you see Lil Cee out here, today?" Asked Ghost.

"Nah... But, someone said he might be a rat." Said Demi.

"He might be a rat?" Said Ghost. *"Do you hear what you saying, Demi G? So, is he or is he not?"* Ghost asked Demi, looking him right in the eyes.

"Look Demi, get in the car right now." Said Ghost. Demi did as he was told.

"Look lil cuz.... You can't help the spread of rumors out here, unless you see the paperwork. The black and white. Do you hear me?" Said Ghost.

"Yeah, but everybody is saying it." Said Demi.

"I don't care what everybody is saying! You're my little guy, let them bitches gossip." Said Ghost. *"If you don't get any proof of what you're saying, then you're the one gossiping just like them bitches."*

"Here in this game, we only go with facts, if you feel a certain type of way about a nigga that's moving funny, you keep that shit to yourself and distance yourself away from that

individual. You don't call that man a rat, without being able to produce the proof."

"Do I make myself clear?" Asked Ghost.

"Yes O.G...." Said Demi G.

"Look Demi, in life I want you to believe half of what you see and none of what you hear. It's easy for a nigga to say something that he might consider weird, and be quick to jump to a conclusion. All it takes is for a nigga to hear a rumor about one of his enemies, and then the next thing you know the rumor is spreading like a wildfire. Now, you have two sides of the story, but there's only one truth. Which is?" Asked Ghost.

"Black and White!" Said Demi.

"Right........ That's right, kid." Said Ghost, happy with the answer Demi gave.

"That's how we get to the bottom of things, Demi G! Now, Lil Cee ain't no rat, the police caught him with some weed on Franklin St..., put him in the cop car and took his around this corner. Brought him back to the projects without any charges pressed on him. Now guess what the projects is going to say?"

"That he's a rat!" Said Demi.

"Exactly.... My point. Lil Cee ain't tell. You think the police out here give a fuck about some weed, when niggas out here getting rich off of crack and dope?"

"Now, that you put it like that......Hell no." said Demi G.

"The police want us to believe that Lil Cee a snitch so that we would exterminate the rat." Ghost explained.

"See, young Demi G, this tactic is called divide and conquer. This is an old trick that the New Haven Police Department have been using since, even before my time. They're all about corruption. They have a hell of a history engaging in foul play. The police don't even trust each other. Listen Demi G, let's just say that I have my hands in the mix with the New Haven Police. Everyone has a price.... Well, almost everyone. Look at the jungle, which is 30 seconds away from Union Ave., the New Haven Police headquarters. Those projects have seen millions come through there weekly during the 80's crack era." Said Ghost.

"Demi G, you can't stand on, and believe rumors said by others, lil cuz. These weak-ass niggas nowadays will talk bad about their own mothers. This is why you can't trust shit; these streets are vicious! Remember this, if you don't remember anything else I say .... Believe half of what you see and none of what you hear."

"They will love you for your popularity and what you got."

"You see all the love I got?" Asked Ghost.

"Yeah, everybody loves you O.G." said Demi G.

146

"That's all-fake love! It's not real! They only love me because of who I am, what I got, and what I can do for them!" Said Ghost.

"The whole city loves you and looks up to you O.G." said Demi G.

"Look Lil cuz, when I went to prison, the city didn't love me then. Some of my so-called family and close friends forgot about me. I had people send me money and flicks that I ain't even expecting shit from. When you're down and out, people only see the worst in you. They will throw your flaws all in your face, just so they can have a reason to turn their backs on you." Said Ghost, as he entered into the jungle from the Union Ave. side. Demi G was just sitting there, silent, soaking up all the knowledge he could from his O.G... Demi G knew Ghost was just trying to prepare him for the streets of the Elm.

Ghost parked his Acura Legend in the parking lot by his store in Clique Green.

"Come on Lil nigga, I want you to meet someone." Said Ghost.

"Who we going to meet?" Asked Demi G, curious of who Ghost was talking about.

"My daughter."

147

"Your daughter? What.... You have a daughter?" Asked Demi G.

"Yeah, I have a daughter, she's around your age. Her mother and I don't get along so she keeps my baby girl away from me due to my relation with her cousin, Candace." Said Ghost.

"It's a long story, but I want you to look over her as your little sister. From time to time, I come here to the Jungle to visit her at Netta's apartment." Said Ghost.

"Wow, you really had a daughter all this time my age? Where she at?" Demi G asked, excited.

"Come on." Said Ghost.

They walked through Diego court until they reached Columbus Ave. Joey Ghost knocked on apartment 104B. Netta came and answered the door.

"Hey Ghost baby." Netta said, in a flirtation tone.

"Hey Netta, where's my baby girl?" Questioned Ghost.

"She's on her way downstairs right now, but anyway, what's up with you tho, Ghost? You still chasing around Sade lil funky ass? You need to come and get some of this good pussy." Said Netta.

Ghost just laughed at Netta's flirtatious comments.

"Girl, you still the same......You ain't never gonna change, Netta." Ghost said, as his daughter came to the door.

"Hey baby girl......Daddy missed you baby."

Ghost barely got the opportunity to see his daughter due to the situation with her mother. So, Ghost had to call a longtime friend to set up a visit between him and his daughter, so she could have playdates with her niece.

"I want you to meet someone." Said Ghost.

Ghost turned around and Demi G was right there, *"Hey, my name is Demi."*

"Hello Demi, my name is Rickita."

Rickita was in love already. Rickita never knew what a crush was until she first laid eyes on Demi G. Rickita just stared at Demi G for about another minute until she asked him how old he was, because even though Demi was only 12 years old, he could pass for about 16. *"How old are you?"* Asked Kita.

"I'm 12, soon to be 13 years old." Said Demi G.

"We the same age, your father told me already." Ghost walked off to holla at his boy Cheese, while Rickita and Demi talked.

"Let's walk to the store in Clique Green."

There was a group of young Jungle brothers coming from the Malcom courts side of the projects. They were mean-mugging Demi G. Demi has been in this situation before, couple years ago in the G.; so he was a little nervous, but definitely wasn't letting it show in front of his new friend, Rickita.

One of the young Jungle brothers threw up the Jungle sign towards Demi G, which was the index finger and the pinky after a bailed-up fist. Each finger represents the sides of the Jungle, Columbus Ave. is the street that splits the projects.

Demi G returned the Hill sign right back at them. The Jungle brother just nodded their heads to let Demi G know that he was good.

"They always on corny shit when they see anyone new in the Jungle." Said Kita.

"Yeah. I could tell that they were on some bullshit, ready for war." Said Demi, as they continued to the store to buy some junk food.

"So, when is the next time I'm going to see you, Demi?" Asked Rickita.

"Well, all the time now, we're like siblings. Your pops told me to look after you like a sister." Said Demi. Rickita was thinking to herself like, *"I don't care what my father said nigga, you belong to me now!"*

She developed a huge crush on Demi G, and no one was going to stop her from being with him.

"Well, I guess, but as long as I get to see you." Said Rickita, not trying to show her crush.

They exchange beeper numbers before Joey Ghost and his man, Cheese, appeared from the South-Orange side of the projects.

"Come on, Demi!!" Yelled Ghost.

"Okay Kita, I'll see you again soon, baby girl. I love you and call me." Yelled Ghost to his daughter.

"O.k. daddy, I'm going to page you later, love." Said Rickita.

Chapter Twenty - One

Lee

Lee was coming from Fair Haven, about to be in town. He had just been notified of the disturbing news about the kidnapping of Miss Edwards, and the murder of Ty-Ty. He had been trying to get in contact with Demi G, but he wasn't answering his phone.

"These Tre niggas about to get it!" Lee said to himself, while his hand rested on his Mack 11.

"These niggas killed my nigga, Ty-Ty" Lee started to cry more and more, as he was reminiscing about their childhood memories together.

Lee parked his car right in the middle of Edgewood Ave. and Kensington St., and got out the car.

Tap, Tap, Tap. Tap……. Tap, Tap, Tap, Tap.

Lee sprayed at a live dice game on Kensington St.

"Y'all niggas fucked with the wrong one." Lee shot, killing two of them. He continued walking down Kensington, making his way towards Chapel St.

Tap, Tap, Tap, Tap. …. Lee was going out in a blaze of glory.

"I'm not going to prison……I'ma be judged right here in these streets! Right here, in the same hood my nigga got murdered in!" Said Lee.

"Y'all niggas want war? Then that's what we gonna do, then!" Tap, Tap, Tap, Tap.

Lee raised his weapon and fired towards the police. Within minutes, the New Haven Police swarmed, building a perimeter around Lee.

Tap, Tap, Tap, Tap!

Lee started moving his way towards the police.

Blocka, Blocka, Blocka, Blocka..........

Lee ducked behind a car as the police bust back.

"Take that, muthafuckas......This is for Ty..."

Before Lee could finish his statement. Blocka! One of the officers caught Lee dead smack in his head as he let off a few more shots from his Mack 11. Lee was pronounced dead on the scene.

- - -

- 1997 -

"Y'all ready to put this work in?" Asked Ghost.

"You already know, O.G." Said Messy.

"I have been ready! Cuz, this what us G-niggas do." Said T-Nice, throwing up the G sign.

This was Demi G's first mission, so he was extra-nervous. It was time to show Joey Ghost that he was ready for whatever. Ghost already showed him how to fire a gun, and also gave him a glock-23 that he always kept close to him.

"Yeah, I'm ready, O.G." Said Demi G.

They pulled off, driving on their way to Waterbury. Ct. Everyone rode in complete silence during the drive. Demi G didn't have the slightest idea where they were on their way to, which really had him super nervous but, right now wasn't the time or place to show it.

He wanted to show the O.G. that he wasn't that average young boy, that he had that killer in him.

Joey Ghost parted the stolen Dodged Caravan on Long Hill Road. They all made sure that their guns were ready to fire and their masks were pulled down. Joey Ghost led the way.

"Look Messy, you stay in the front just in case they try to run out the front door."

"T-Nice, you stay in the back for the same reason……. Demi G, you stay with me." Said Ghost.

All three young goons nodded their heads in agreement. Joey Ghost and Demi G crept on the side of the four-story building, jumping up on the fire escape, climbing until they reached the third floor.

"Now look.... You see this window that's cracked. I'ma go in first, you make sure you watch my back as I go in. You got it, youngin?" Said Ghost.

"Yeah, O.K........ I got you O.G." said Demi G.

Joey Ghost made his way through the window. The room was empty, all that was in the room was a bunch of empty Budweiser cans. Joey Ghost crept to the room door and cracked it open. He heard nothing.

He waved at Demi G, *"Come on, lil cuz........ The coast is clear."* Said Ghost. Demi G climbed through the windows in no time.

Joey Ghost and Demi G crept down the hallway of the third floor of the building. Everything was still a standstill....... Quiet. The third floor was cleared, so, they decide to make their way to the second floor.

"Look Demi, stay right behind me, I could hear someone speaking in Spanish." Ghost knew it was go-time.

"Come on." Ghost ordered.

Joey Ghost could hear what sounded like three Mexicans, talking to each other in one room and two in the other room.

"Look Demi, I need you to go downstairs to make sure no one is down there, it sounds like it's five of them altogether, so, we only have four to worry about." Said Ghost.

155

"Hold up.........I thought you said it's five Mexicans altogether, so why do we have to only worry about four?" Demi G asked confused.

"Lil nigga, I know what I said. One of them is my girl. The one black person in here is my girl. So, we gonna kill the four Mexicans." Said Ghost.

Demi G knew there was a lot more to the story, but right now wasn't the time to be asking questions. All that mattered right now was to show his loyalty to Ghost. Demi did as he was told and crept downstairs. No one was down there. He looked in the front window to see if Messy was on post, which he was, like the true soldier he was. Demi Fantasized about smoking Messy, but he knew he couldn't, cause O.G. really had genuine love for him.

Demi G flew back to the second floor.

"O.G. it's clear downstairs." Said Demi G.

"O.k., come on." Ghost said to Demi G, as they drew their guns and made their way to the room with the three in it.

"O.G., should I go to the other room?" Asked Demi G.

"NO! come with me and do what I say!"

BOOM!!! Ghost kicked down the door. Blocka, Blocka, Blocka....... Ghost shot the Mexican in the head that was sitting by the door, snorting cocaine up his nose, while Demi had one Mexican at gunpoint in the corner with his Glock.

156

"No No......Don't shoot me!" The Mexican screamed out.

Demi just stood there, stuck-pointing his gun, knowing that he never shot anyone before in his life.

Demi thought to himself, *"Damn, do I really have the courage to murder this Mexican."*

Joey Ghost ran after the third Mexican.

Someone in the back of the house had fired a single shot. BLOCKA! Demi didn't know who had fired the shot. The Mexican was still begging for his life. Demi G just stared, squeezing the handle, petrified to pull the trigger.

The third Mexican ran out the front door.... Blocka, Blocka! Messy was right there waiting on him. The Mexican's brains flew everywhere.

With the 357. Mag, Messy stood over him.... Y'all Mexicans thought y'all could come over here and take our money, right? I finally got one of y'all motherfuckers! Now, look at you. With your fucking head split in half.......... Rest In Peace." Said Messy, talking to the dead Mexican.

Demi was still standing there like a mannequin with his pistol pointed to the Mexican. Joey came behind Demi and placed his hand on his shoulder.

"Look, lil cuz, it's time to bust your cherry."

Demi looked up at Joey Ghost and squeezed......Blocka, Blocka, Blocka! "You right, O.G." said Demi G.

Sade came out of one of the other rooms in the back, with a big trash-bag, and also with her 9mm in her hand.

"I got it, baby." Said Sade.

T-Nice was mad as hell, as he didn't get any action. He came upstairs to make sure everything was clear.

"Come on......We have to be out before them people show up."

Demi G was still in a state of shock, because he just murdered someone. All types of thoughts were running through his head.

Joey Ghost walked over to Demi G and said, "That's how I was when I caught my first body, now, let's get moving, lil cuz."

"O.K., O.G." said Demi G.

As they were all going to get in the van, Messy was still over the dead body, talking to it.

"Ayo Messy, nigga come in!" Yelled Ghost.

"Hold up, O.G., I'm talking to the dead." Said Messy. Everybody just shook their heads.

Demi G thought to himself, *"This nigga is crazy as fuck, and was wondering what was in that trash-bag that was full of whatever it was."*

He decided not to ask any questions. Demi G realized that this whole thing was a set-up when he saw that Sade was part of the plot.

She had to kill that Mexican that was in that other room, at the back, which would explain where that single gunshot came from. The very next morning, Demi G was exhausted due to getting very little sleep.

Taking someone's life was weighing heavy on his conscience.

Demi G walked out of his aunt, Lanisha's apartment, in the G to meet Joey Ghost on the Franklin St. side.

"What's up, lil cuz?" Said Ghost.

"I'm cooling, O.G., what's good with you?" Said Demi G.

"You know me, lil cuz, just another day." Ghost replied Demi G.

"It feels weird O.G......I'm not gonna lie to you. I'm confused, that shit ain't make any sense to me." Said Demi G.

"Because it's not supposed to make any sense to you! Look, lil cuz... Life is like a game of chess. In chess, you have a King, a Queen, Bishops, Knights, Rooks, and Pawns. Everyone in life plays a position, and every time you make a chess move, you make sure it's a defensive move, as well as an offensive

move; so that way, it's like you're making two moves at once."
Said Ghost.

"Pawns are meant to be sacrificed for a greater purpose. But once a pawn gets all the way down the field, it earns a higher position. What will a pawn ever become?" Asked Ghost.

"The King." Demi G replied.

"Exactly! .... A king sits on his throne and watches the battlefield, calling all the shots. The entire time, no one really knows what's on the King's agenda." Said Ghost.

"Listen kid, get in the car, we going to take a ride across town. I gotta go to the Ville on Read St. I want you to meet my lil nigga, G-Bo."

Chapter Twenty - Two

1998

Downtown, New Haven on Crown St., was the club called 'The Alley Cat.' Every Thursday was youth night, between ages 14 to 18 years old.

All the hoods in the Elm come out on Thursday nights. All the Chicks and Young niggas was fresh to death. This was the time to see what hood was the flyest, what hood was the hardest, and what hood was getting the most money.

Demi G and all the Ghetto Boys was in line about to pay $10 to get in the club. The Ghetto Boys was known to be the flyest. They were about 25 deep when they finally entered the club. The music was blasting. All you could see was all types of neighborhood gang signs in the air.

Demi G saw all the H.I.V. niggas, crowded together like an army. They were always deep. The Hill, Island, and Ville niggas. You could even see some niggas with H.I.V. sprayed on the front of their shirts. And on the other side of the club was the T.N.T. niggas accompanied by the Ghetto Boys.

Both sides were just grilling each other, throwing up their signs; while Jay-z and D.M.X.'s, 'More money, more cash, more hoes, was bumping through the speakers.'

Demi G looked at the juice bar and saw a beautiful face that looked familiar. It was Nue. He loved running into Nue in public. Anytime he saw Nue, he always admired and appreciated her beauty. Demi G walked over to the juice bar.

"Hey Nue." Said Demi G.

"Hey Boo-Boo." Nue said, calling Demi G the nickname she gave him back in summer camp days. They gave each other a hug.

"Who are you here with?" Said Nue

"I'm here with the Ghetto Boys." Said Demi G.

"But ain't you from the Hill?"

"Yeah, I'm from the Hill." Said Demi G.

"So, why aren't you over there with the H.I.V. niggas? You playing a dangerous game, ain't you Demi?" Said Nue, concerned about the safety of her friend."

"These young niggas don't understand none of that, and right now it looks like you with G-niggas." Said Nue.

"Ayo cuz, what's up? You need to come over with us!" Screamed Messy, trying to be loud over the speakers.

Messy had his kills-grill on his face, throwing up the Ghetto sign with both hands in the air. *"Naw, I'm cool right here, my nigga."* Said Demi G, as he looked over where the Hill niggas was. They were all looking at him, shaking their heads whispering to one another. They started throwing up the Hill sign at him.

"What hood you repping my nigga?" Messy asked Demi G, while staring at him dead in the eyes.

"Look cuz, I'm from the Hill, but I'm repping this money!" Said Demi G.

"Look…. Cuz, that shit sounds good, but this is the Elm City, Nigga! So whoever you getting money with, thats's the hood you repping Nigga!" Said Messy, before he walked back over to his T.N.T. niggas.

"Boo-Boo, all this shit is corny. Why can't we all just get along…" Said Nue.

"I can't wait till I'm far away from here, in modeling school. You're too smart to be a part of this bull-shit, Demi." Said Nue, shaking her head.

Demi got into a deep thought about all this neighborhood beef, and felt like all this beef-shit was a bunch of nonsense. A familiar face came out of the H.I.V. crowd, and Demi G was all smiles. To his surprise of seeing his best friend, Nashawn.

"What's up, nigga. Where you from, nigga?" Nashawn said, playing around.

"The Hill! All day!" Said Demi G.

Nashawn was one of the best basketball players in the Elm, even at the age of 14 years old.

He was a 6'1 freshman at James Hill-house, who played the Point-Guard position on the Varsity squad. He was already receiving scholarship letters from division one colleges.

Summertime leagues banned him from playing in the Elm City. Nashawn earned the name, Greatness, through his basketball talent. But, there was another side of Greatness that only some of his close friends around the Hill North knew about. Greatness has an evil side to him, and he's with all the bull-shit and whatever comes with it.

"Ayo kid, you're my day-one and I'm riding with you, regardless of what a nigga might think, but you need to make up your mind with who you're with, because our hood thinks you're running with those G-niggas." Said Greatness.

"Look cuz, whenever you come back to the hood, get at me so I can put niggas in their places, or I'm coming down to Ms. Edward's crib!" Said Greatness, then walked back to his H.I.V. crowd. Demi G turned back around and continued his conversation with Nue, about his poor decision making. Demi hated when Nue was on his line with all the holy talk. She made Demi feel like she was his second mother.

- - -

- Three months Later -

Demi G was in the Hill, in front of Leon's, with his Cuban link chain on, with an ice-out Jesus' head medallion, when Dark-skin Jack drove by.

Dark-skin Jack ran almost the whole Hill. He's from Davenport Ave. If you wanted or needed anything, you had to go through Dark-skin Jack. Jack was a 5'10 cubby nigga. Always fly and was as black as midnight. He was rich off the streets of the Elm City. A real big homie of the Hill, and the D.P.P. crew. Everybody loved and looked up to him.

Dark skin Jack busted a U-Turn once he saw Demi G, and parked right in front of Leon's.

"What's up, cuz?" Said Dark-Skin Jack.

"Shit, just chilling cuz." Said Demi G.

"You ready to get some real Hill money? That Davenport blood money?" Said Jack.

"I'm already getting money." Said Demi G. Dark-skin Jack pulled out $10,000 and flashed it in front of Demi G's face.

"Nigga you ain't seeing no real money in those projects. I just picked these 10 bands up from down the street, that was made within the last two hours, nigga." Said Jack

"You and whoever you work them packs for, ain't getting no real paper like this, cuz. This is the Hill!" Said Jack, as he threw up the Hill sign.

"Yeah, I heard about you being in those projects with niggas that we don't fuck with." Said Jack.

"Listen, lil cuz. Whenever you ready to leave them clown-ass G-niggas alone, and ready to touch some real bread, let me know. I want you to work for me, and I'ma give you Davenport Ave. I'ma make you the head of the D.P.P. Let me know, lil nigga." Said Dark-Skin Jack, as he hopped in his Benz and sped off.

Demi was like *"Damn, he's going to give me all this?"* as he looked up and down Davenport and get down with the notorious D.P.P. Demi G turned around to go back towards his house on Stevens St. He was almost to the corner....... CRACKKK!

A group of young boys from Davenport Ave. was beating the hell out of Demi G. One young boy grabbed and punched Demi G right out of his chains.

"Yeah......... Nigga, you want to be a Ghetto Boy, huh?" One of his little Hill niggas said.

One of the other Hill niggas yelled out, "This a Hill beat down! Punk-ass nigga."

Demi tried to the best of his ability to break free, but it was about 6 of them jumping him.

Greatness was walking down Stevens St., towards Davenport, to the sight of his best friend getting the ass-whooping of his life. Greatness pulled out his P-95 45. Cal Ruger and smacked the first nigga that was the closest to him right in the face. SMACK!!! Blocka, Blocka, Blocka

Greatness let off three shots in the air, to let them know he wasn't playing. All the young niggas from Davenport Ave. just froze.

"Get the fuck up off my nigga!!" Greatness screamed. Demi G was bleeding from his nose, shirt all ripped up, and no chain around his neck.

"This nigga from the G." One of them yelled.

"No, the fuck he ain't! He's from right here, just like the rest of us! He's a Hill nigga." Said Greatness.

Greatness pointed the 45 at them and said, "Give him his chain back before I put a bullet in your face." They did as Greatness ordered.

Demi was pissed to the max! He wanted to grab the gun out of Greatness' hand and shoot all of them right there.

"Come on, Demi G, we gotta clean you cuz. They beat the shit out of you!" Greatness said, while laughing at the same

time. All the Davenport niggas left disappointed. Greatness most definitely fucked up their little situation. Greatness had all the young niggas in his age bracket shook of him.

One of the young boys told Demi G. *"We will see you again!"*

Greatness walked Demi G. to Ms. Edwards so he could change clothes and clean himself up.

"Nigga, I told you this day was going to come. They were giving you the Hill beat down." Great said, while laughing again.

"Shut the fuck up Nashawn! This shit ain't funny."

"Look cuz, I'm about to start up my own gang called S.S.G. (Segal St gang), get down with me cuz!" Said Greatness.

"What happened to Stevens St. Posse?" Asked Demi.

"Segal St. gang is the younger version of S.S.P....... I know you fuck with Joey Ghost and them G-niggas, but this is your home, cuz and you will be a good fit for us. We need you, bro! We taking hits and catching licks!" Said Greatness.

"What about your basketball career?" Asked Demi

"I'm always going to play ball, that will never change. But right now, I need to eat! I need money!" Said Greatness.

"I was just thinking about the offer Dark-Skin Jack proposed to me, right before I got jumped by them dirty-ass niggas." Said Demi.

"Dark-Skin Jack?" Greatness yelled out.

"Man, I wouldn't be surprised if he was the one who called the shot for you to get jumped." Said Greatness.

"As soon as he pulled off, they were on my ass!" Said Demi.

"Listen bro, your day was coming anyway, whether he was behind it or not......Because you be fucking with them G-niggas. Look cuz. You are a Hill nigga. Fuck them G-niggas!" Greatness said.

"Come fuck with us, Segal St. niggas. We about to take over!" Greatness said, while flashing his heat.

Chapter Twenty - Three

1999

Demi G finally stopped fucking with the Ghetto Boys because he realized he's a Hill nigga, and decided he was ready to get down with Dark-Skin Jack, and take him up on his offer.

Demi just stopped answering Ghost's phone calls, and even changed his beeper number. Ghost was in his Acura cruising down Stevens St., hoping to bump into Demi G. He missed his little guy and was wondering what he was up to.

Greatness saw Joey Ghost's Acura while he was sitting on his porch and waved him down.

Ghost pulled over and rolled down his window. Greatness walked off the porch, and went to Ghost's window.

"O.G., I got to holla at you." Greatness said.

"Aight, hop in .... Where's my young God?" Asked Ghost, curious if Greatness Knew Demi G's whereabouts.

"Oh man...... Cuz did some bullshit! He went and got down with that nigga, Dark-Skin Jack on Davenport Ave. up the block. He gave Demi the whole block. FUCK DEMI!" Said Greatness.

Greatness was angry that Demi G didn't want to get down with Segal St. gang, and he was getting to a bag. Demi G was making more money in the Hill, than he ever made in the G. There weren't any comparisons.

Joey Ghost was upset to hear this news. He just wasn't trying to show it to Greatness.

"Joey Ghost I'm telling you right now, anything you need me to do, I got you." Said Greatness.

"Me and my Segal St. niggas are on straight bullshit, give me the green light, and I'll have Demi G parked." Said Greatness.

"Nah, you don't kill Demi." Said Ghost. "But, I want to meet the rest of your gang."

"Look, how often does Dark-Skin Jack come through Davenport Ave.?" Asked Joey Ghost.

"Shit. He's always posted on Ann St., with Dee Gotti and niggas, so he's in the hood all the time." Said Greatness.

"O.K., do you got his beeper number?"

"Yeah, that's my old head." Greatness said.

"O.k, I'ma hit you later tonight around 10 p.m. You now work for me. You and your Segal St. gang are now on my payroll. We need Demi G back." Said Ghost.

"Man, fuck Demi G. He's a bitch." Said Greatness.

171

"Demi is a boss in the making, and full of potential, you don't kill niggas like him." Said Ghost.

"You just meet me back here at 10 p.m. tonight."

- - -

- Later that night -

Joey Ghost and G-Bo met Greatness on Orchard St. in the Hill.

"Look lil cuz, this is my lil man from Read St. in the Ville." Said Ghost, introducing Greatness to one of his young wolves.

"What's cracking, cuz, I'm G-Bo, how you?" Said G-Bo.

"I'm Greatness, the general of the Segal St. gang." Said Greatness.

"O.K., now that y'all met, both of y'all cliques are under my payroll for now!" Said Ghost.

"And no one should know of this. Greatness you're always screaming the gang-gang shit... Well, I know what my little nigga, G-Bo and his Read St. crew is about...What is you and your Segal St. gang about? That's the question!" Said Ghost.

"O.k., you said Dark-Skin Jack on Ann st.?" Joey Ghost had asked Greatness.

"Yeah, he's always over there at the park. I just know I saw his Benz parked over there." Said Greatness.

"O.k. bet ……. You and G-Bo about to go and handle him right now!" Ghost ordered.

Ghost knew this was the perfect opportunity to finally take over the Hill, and make Demi God the boss all throughout the Hill. Greatness and G-Bo was at the ninja spot till about 11 p.m. when everybody on Ann St. started to leave out. Ann St. is like a safe haven in the Hill North, where all the hustlers in the Hill North just chill and play dice and relax, while their spots made that paper.

"Ayo cuz, as soon as that white Benz drives off, we're going to gun it down." Said Greatness.

They were in the parking lot, on West St. in the projects, right behind Uncle Joe's apartment. Soon after, everybody was leaving, Dark-Skin Jack and his girlfriend got into his Benz. G-Bo and Greatness walked towards Ann St. when they saw the headlights of the Benz come on. Dark-Skin Jack pulled off to meet two masked men with hoodies on throwing bullets at him.

BLOCKA, BLOCKA, BLOCKA, BLOCKA …………

The first bullets fired hit Dark-Skin Jack right in the face, causing him to lose control of his Benz and crash into a parked car.

173

"He's dead, come on! Greatness, we out, cuz!" Said G-Bo.

"Nah cuz, word to D-Lover it ain't over." Greatness said, and ran to the car and put a hole in Dark-Skin Jack's girlfriend's head. They ran around to the driver's side to make sure that Dark-Skin Jack was dead!

BLOCKA. BLOCKA, BLOCKA, BLOCKA! Putting 4 holes also in his head. *"Now, we done!"* Said Greatness.

Chapter Twenty - Four

2000

Demi G's aunt, Lanisha, was driving up Congress Ave., when she ran into her nephew, Demi.

"Hey, lil nigga, come over here." Said Lanisha.

Demi G was in front of the store, in the Hill that everyone calls the 24, where all the local hustlers posted up in front of, selling their dime bags of crack. Word on the street was that Dark-Skin Jack and his bitch got caught slipping by some niggas from the Tre, at least that's what the rumor was. Anytime a Hill nigga gets smoked unexpectedly, people automatically believe Tre niggas had something to do with it. That's just how it's always been.

"Hey aunty Nene, what you doing around here?" Asked Demi G.

"Nigga......If you don't get your lil ugly-ass out of here. Talking bout what am I doing around here! This was my hood before you were even thought of." Said Lanisha.

"But anyway, Ghost been looking for you. He told me to tell you to come to the projects to see him." Said Lanisha.

"Nah......I'll pass! I'm from the Hill and it's D.P.P. for life" said Demi G.

175

"Nigga, you sound like you look! Dumb and broke. Hanging around all these damn bums around here. Since Dark-Skin Jack got murdered. Y'all niggas out here looking hungry as hell." Said Lanisha.

"Where's your chain at?" Asked Lanisha

"I sold it." Said Demi.

"Damn, You are doing bad my nigga! All them lover's cut niggas right there in the lover's parking lot getting all that money, while you are over here getting crumbs from all the fiends that's coming short." Said Lanisha.

"Get your ass in this car right now before I get out and drag your ass in this car!"

"Aunty......I'm not going back to those projects! I'm a Hill nigga. These are my niggas." Said Demi G.

"Look nephew, shit is bigger than some neighborhood, much bigger!" Said Lanisha.

Demi G really didn't want to face Joey Ghost after he stopped fucking with him. But, now Joey Ghost had requested to see him in person.

"O.K., aunty, I'm coming right now." Demi said, then ran over to Big Ether to grab his Glock 40 off him. Demi hopped in his aunt's car. *"Let's go, aunty Nene."*

As they entered the projects from the Franklin St. side, all the little niggas from the G just stared at Demi G through the window of the car.

Some was even throwing up the G-sign at him. Demi G returned the Hill sign back at them. Demi knew as long as Joey Ghost was alive, he had a pass to the Ghetto.

Joey Ghost was standing right outside his brand new 2000 Range Rover. He was looking at Demi, clapping his hands.

"Hey Demi God, congrats on you being the boss over there on the north now." Said Joey Ghost.

"What are you talking about?" Asked Demi. Demi knew he was broke as fuck! He was struggling just to get by day-to-day.

"I'm talking about you leaving me to go over there to be the man! You have to step your game up, kid!"

"Do you see what happens when your King is checkmated? You and your Davenport niggas are broke, looking for a home!" Ghost said.

"Look. I'm home Demi, always have been." Joey Ghost said, getting closer to Demi. *"You just got caught up in your neighborhood drama. It ain't your fault, young king."*

"The drug game is bigger than what you think. A lot bigger. I just recently took over majority of the Elm City. it's just

177

one section that I haven't conquered, and that's the Hill where you from."

"Listen Demi, I'ma front you half-a-key every two weeks. You bust it down and give it to your niggas just like you did when you were over here hustling on the Hamilton side. Whenever someone needs to purchase some weight, they'll go through you, and you'll got a percentage of the play." Said Joey Ghost. Demi G was shocked.

"So basically, I will be the boss over there?" Asked Demi.

"Yes! You were born to be a boss! Now it's time to show the world what you're made off. Look over there, young king." Ghost said pointing to the Acura Legend.

"That's yours now." Said Ghost.

"Hell nooo! For real? Dam, thanks O.G." Demi G said as he ran over to his first car. A 1996 Acura Legend.

"They don't make these anymore, 1996 was the last year Acura made the Legend. So it's real special." Said Ghost.

Ghost threw Demi the keys. Don't fuck it up, kid, treat it as if it a brand-new Benz.

Joey Ghost walked over to Lanisha. *"Hey Nisha, do you think he's ready?"*

"Yes." Said Lanisha.

"He got all the potential! Watch my nephew going to have the Hill North in a headlock!"

- - -

- Present -

"Y'all bitch-ass niggas going to die." Said Ms. Edwards.

"Shut the fuck up! Your son is a bitch......A bitch with money," said Nasty.

Greatness and G-Bo are going to be proud of us. "Your sucker-ass son is about to pull up with a half a mill for your old ass!" Said Olee. Black Flag gang had Ms. Edwards tied up to a chair on Sheffield Ave. in the Ville, waiting on the call from the big homies, Greatness and G-Bo.

"I really want to shoot this old bitch in her head!" Said Nasty.

"Then we ain't going to have any money, Stupid." Said Olee. Mary came, waiting in the room looking so sexy in her black lace cat-suit.

"Bitch, I never trusted you. I knew you were a little trifling whore! My son is too good for you, and you know it!" Said Ms. Edwards.

"Someone stick a dirty sock in this bitch's mouth A.S.A.P.!" Said Mary. Olee did as she said and put a sock in Ms. Edward mouth.

"Look bitch, your son is what we call a male pussy! He's a bitch......How does it feel to raise a bitch? That's the reason why he never tasted this pussy. This, right here..." said Mary, as she waved her black bandana in the air.

"This is what gets my pussy wet! You worth $500,000 to us right now! And I bet you didn't know that your son was part of a Mexican cartel! His bitch-ass should have stayed in Yale." Said Mary.

Mary turned around struggling to pull down her cat-suit. Once she finally got the tight one-piece to her knees, she showed Ms. Edwards the big tattoo on her ass that read, "Nashawn!" in big bold letter.

"This is Greatness' big fat ass! If your son would've got some of this pussy, he would've been seen this tat. I had it for just about a year now." Said Mary.

Ms. Edwards was shaking her head, and mumbling with tears in her eyes, wondering how her son was so intelligent and stupid at the same time.

Greatness and G-Bo walked in the door, Mary ran and jumped into Greatness' arms, tonguing him down.

"Did you make that call yet, baby?" Said Greatness.

"Yes Nashawn, he should definitely know by now that the ransom is $500,000. I put the word out to his H.B.O. niggas." Said Mary.

Listening to Mary's words, and seeing her son betrayed by his best friend had the tears falling rapidly down Ms Edward's face.

Chapter Twenty - Five

2002.... Mary

Mary walked into school at James Hill-house, looking beautiful as usual when the school bell rung. She bumped into Greatness in the hallway.

"Hey baby!" Greatness said, as Mary looked all around her to see if anybody heard what Greatness just called her.

"Hey Nashawn."

"So, all I get is a hey?" Asked Greatness.

"Bitch, don't make me slap the shit out of you in the school! And you better not be trying to give Demi G no pussy either!" Said Greatness.

"I'm not." Said Mary.

"Fuck that bitch-ass nigga! Segal St. niggas ain't playing with no one!" Said Greatness.

"Segal street, ALL DAY EVERYDAY!" Said Mary. Greatness and Mary always had a secret relationship behind Demi's back.

Mary fell in love with Greatness all because of how popular he was in high school. Everybody loved Greatness due to his basketball-playing abilities. He had all the potentials to get to the

N.B.A., and rumor has it that he'll be going straight to the league right out of high school.

So, Mary felt like she had to give Greatness some pussy, so when he made it big, he wouldn't forget about her.

"You make sure you beep me as soon as you leave school." Said Greatness.

"O.K., baby." Mary said, looking in both directions to make sure no one was around to listen.

A few months ago, after Mary was leaving Demi's house on Stevens St., Greatness stopped her. He asked her what did she see in Demi. Mary replied "He's handsome, dark, polite and he's getting money."

"So, you telling me that I'm not handsome, polite and getting money?" Asked Greatness.

"Shit, I'm on my way to the N.B.A."

"Ain't that your best friend? He speaks so highly of you." Said Mary.

"Yea, that's my friend but fuck him! I need you in my life, plus he fucks with that model bitch from the Tribe." Said Greatness.

"Yeah, her name is Nue." Said Greatness.

"Oh shit, that's the girl he grew up with. Nue from the Tribe." Said Mary.

"Look you ain't no fucking-angel either! You been fucking with older niggas anyway, so don't act like you some type of virgin or something. Listen, you my bitch now! And you better not give that nigga no ass!" Said Greatness. Mary came back to reality.

"O.k., I'ma beep you as soon as I leave here. Don't you have basketball practice?" Mary said, being arrogant.

Chapter Twenty - Six

Demi G

Demi G had tears in his eyes as he got off exit 44. He noticed that he had several missed calls from Lee. Demi G had a gut feeling that Ty-Ty getting murdered, and his mother's kidnapping was retaliation for something that had to do with Joey Ghost or Greatness.

Tre niggas had killed Ty-Ty in revenge for Black and Dawg, who Greatness murdered for Joey Ghost, but why would Joey Ghost have Black and Dawg smoked in the first place? That was the question that was pondering in Demi's head.

Demi G found out through Chuyloco, that Black and Dawg was working for him. But it wasn't a robbery! It was an assassination; they died with 18 kilos of pure cocaine on them. The whole entire time Joey Ghost knew and kept it between him and Greatness. Demi thought to himself, why would Ghost put a whole act like he had nothing to do with the hit that was really going on?

Demi G looked down at his phone and saw another missed call from Killa Jay, Demi G called the number back.

"What's cracking, Killa Jay?"

"Ayo cuz, it's mad shit going on right now! Them Black Flag niggas got your mom and they are asking for $500,000 for

her ransom, and Ty-Ty and Lee got smoked in the Tre." Said Killa Jay.

"Word to D-Lover cuz, we're on it right now. We bout to go slide on them Read St. niggas for your mom." Said Killa Jay, ready to ride for his friend.

"Alright bet... I'm on Ella-Grasso right now, on my way to pick up the bread to get my mom back!" Said Demi G.

"Ayo cuz. You won't believe who was the one that called me for the money!" Said Killa Jay.

"Who?" Asked Demi G.

"Mary cuz......Real Shit bro!"

"Damn, for real cuz?" Asked Demi G, as he was shaking his head side-to-side. His feeling was crushed!

"Before she hung up, she said Black Flag, Money Bags." Said Killa Jay.

"Demi, Demi?" Killa Jay called out Demi's name

Demi was spaced-out for a second. *"Yo, yo, yo."* Said Demi, snapping back to reality.

"Listen cuz. Fuck that bitch! She ain't shit, but a whore anyway!" Said Killa Jay.

"Yeah bro, you're right!" Said Demi G.

"She helped line my mom up! I'm showing no mercy! Everyone that's involved has a hollow tip in my clip with their name on it!" Demi G said, crying.

Demi G had nothing but murder on his mind. All he could see is the color red.

"Ayo cuz, get the whole H.B.O. ready! We going to show the Elm City who runs this bitch! It's about to be a 'nightmare in the Elm City'." Said Demi G, with a devilish smile on his face.

"After I get my mom back, Tre niggas, Black Flag Gang, Ghetto boys, and anyone else that's affiliated with them Segal St. niggas going to feel my pain." Demi G said, before hanging up his phone. Demi G dialed the number of his uncle, Fred.

Uncle Fred was an old school Hill nigga, that was from the Bridge. He jumped out of the game and went strictly legit. He owned all types of different businesses.

"Uncle Fred, what's up?" Said Demi G.

"Hey lil nigga, I been blowing your phone up, neph!" Said Uncle Fred.

"Yeah, I know unc. I been running like crazy." Said Demi G.

"The whole town talking about my sister being kidnapped! And they're asking for half a mil......Nephew, what the fuck you got your mother into?" Said Uncle Fred.

187

"Unc.... Not right now! Open the door, I'm about to pull-up right now!" Said Demi G.

Demi G pulled to Uncle Fred's house on Ward St. Demi G jumped out of his 745 Beemer. Uncle Fred greeted him at the front door.

"Ayo Uncle Fred, if something happens to her...... I'ma lose it! I don't know what to do right now!" Said Demi G.

"Come into the house, nephew. Now, first thing is getting your mom back safe!" Said Uncle Fred.

"I'm on it A.S.A.P. .... I'ma need you to grab $500,000 out of the safe!" Said Demi G.

"I already got it out. It's right here. When I first heard what happened I grabbed it out the stash, Demi."

"Unc thanks." Demi G said, as he turned around to speed out the door.

"Hold up lil nigga, let me holla at you... I know you're feeling like you been betrayed by everyone and people you loved. Demi, I want you to know the day you decided to jump into this game, you were betrayed! This game doesn't love you, nephew. The game's foundation was built upon betrayal! Everything you going through right now, the game was designed for you to go through it. Right now, nephew, you have to be strong. Not only for you, but for your mother. This is the time for you to put your

emotions to the side and put your brain into play. Remember what I always used to tell you as a little boy……Intelligence over emotions! Emotions will take you places, but intelligence will take you where you need to be!" Said Uncle Fred. pointing with his index finger to Demi's head.

Demi G was just staring at his uncle.

"Now, take this money and go get my sister. I also took out another $100,000 of your money just in case things go south and you need to go on the run! Don't come back here where the rest of your bread and drugs are. They might be watching right now. I'm talking about the Feds." Said Uncle Fred, as he walked over the cabinet.

Uncle Fred grabbed a level 5 bulletproof vest and a pair of 9mm Berettas, with 30 round extended clips and handed them to Demi.

"Now, go and get your mother! And Demi remember, think with your head, not your emotions." Said Uncle Fred.

"Okay… Love you Unc." Said Demi G, before leaving out the door.

Demi G hopped back into his 745 and called Killa Jay back.

"Ayo cuz, did she tell you the location of the meet?" Asked Demi G. "Yea of course, I was just waiting on the call from you." Said Killa Jay.

"They said in the Tre-deuce, on the corner of Ellsworth and Elm St..., have the half a mil there at 11 p.m. sharp or she's dead!" Said Killa Jay, with sadness in his voice.

"Cuz we're on it right now, locked and ready! We about 40 deep right now!"

"Look cuz, stand down right now!" Demi G ordered.

"Say less big cuz! We'll be waiting on your call to move out!" Said Killa Jay.

"We about to blow this city up as soon as I get my mom back.... And I have a few personal situations I need to do!" Said Demi G, referring to Greatness and Mary.

"Ayo, one last thing before we hang up.... The streets are saying that you murdered Lunatic! We don't need them hearing that, then they repay the favor with your mom dukes." Said Killa Jay

"Nah......Don't worry about that! As long as I have this $500,000 my mom will be safe! Those Black Flag niggas are too thirsty and broke to do some dumb-shit like smoke my mom." Said Demi G, with confidence.

"H.B.O...." said Demi G.

"You already know!" Said Killa Jay.

Demi hung up the phone and popped Big Ether new mixtape in the CD deck.

"I'm so fucking Elm City/Hell City/Where the shells get dropped/ The good die young. And the holes on the barrels is hot/

I love my strip/ love West/. Love my bitch/

Trying play me like bouncer. You could love my grip /Around for the smoke could get it all. Suck my dick/

I fuck with Philly. These niggas on some nut ass shit/

I fuck with Jers/ I'm thorough I don't fuck with herbs/

I hate the fakes kill em/ and erase the fakes/ I hate the rats.

Fuck them, and I hate the jakes/ Divide and conquer nigga is

You blood or you grape/ I hate this game, hate how bitch niggas alive/ And ever since Marky- D died. It ain't the same in the Tribe/ I love this city, sometimes a nigga hates this shit/ More funerals they gripping at the wake and shit/I love my hood sometimes, I love my side/ I wish Coov lived and Tymac ain't die/ When p.j. left Daryl made a promise to slide/ he said Big Ether I ain't stopping till I'm dead or they die/ I love my nigga Scavy. I love my clique/Last of a dying breed, you better love this shit/ I'm just a fat black nigga/ that's quick to smoke niggas/Trash niggas/ Back when Bez had the couple AC niggas/ then Vic and Dream first started/ My niggas brave hearted/All out the game that's equipped to save artist/ Aim on point make a nigga shave targets/Ain't no need to talk. Niggas know that we the hardest/ They know that we the best niggas made by us/ Get him picked on a Wednesday like the woman he crush/ close the club and stuff/ Dough tie up the bitch/Ride out like I'm Oomi when he ripping the clutch/ Niggas barely even giving a fuck/No plan. Life sucks/ And all these niggas are stuck."

Chapter Twenty - Seven

Later that night

Demi G decided it was best to go and grab his mother solo. He drove his Acura Legend because it was a dark color and looked black at night. His white Beemer would have stuck out like a sore thumb. The street was so quiet, you could hear a dime drop. Demi G parked on Maple St. Just up the block from Elm St. off of Ellsworth.

Demi G got out of his whip, carrying the duffel bag with the $500,000 in it. Demi G had already circled the block multiple times making sure it wasn't a set-up.

Demi was all alone on the corner before he received a text from Mary which read... *"This is the first lady of the Black Flag Gang, Mary. I'm staring dead at you, drop the money and leave it on the corner."*

Demi G texted back, *"Where's my mother at? I need to see her before I give you the money."*

Mary called Demi G's phone... *"Listen nigga, shut the fuck up before I put a bullet in this bitch's head! Now, do as I say and put the fucking money on the corner and walk away!"*

"Damn Mary, I can't believe you talking to me like this! And you kidnapped my mom!" Said Demi G, with hurt in his voice.

"Yeah nigga... You better believe it! You're a soft-ass nigga and you know it!" Said Mary.

Demi G did as she ordered him to do. He walked three houses up Elm St. towards Ella Grasso before turning around to the sight of the duffel bag gone. Demi G now thought that this was a set-up because the money was gone and he still didn't have his mother back. Demi G pulled both of his nines out ready to hit anything that was moving....... Then all of a sudden Demi G heard something that sounds like mumbling coming from the backyard of the third house down.

Demi G crept quietly ready to put all 60 rounds into someone.

The further he kept creeping down the driveway, the louder the mumbling grew.

"Ohhh shit......Mom!" Demi G yelled out. Tears flowing happy to see his mother.

"I'm sorry mom! I'm so sorry mom! I love you so much!" Demi G, gently removed the duct tape off of her mouth.

"Boy, get me home now!" Said Ms. Edwards.

"Mom, I promise you, they're going to die over this, all of them." said Demi G.

"They better! Every last one of them. Especially that nasty-ass slut Mary! You know that heifer had the damn nerve to pull her pants down and show me her ass? The bitch got

194

'Nashawn' tattooed on her ass!" Said Ms. Edwards. Demi G paused for a second.

"Hold up... You said she had what on her ass?" Demi G just shook his head.

"Forget her mom. I'm not taking you home. Your stuff is packed. Aunt Rose and Aunt Ann are taking you to Florence, South Carolina first thing in the morning. This city is about to blow up!" Said Demi G.

- - -

- 2004 -

Demi G been playing off the radar and haven't been seen in months. He was now in a full-fledged relationship with his girlfriend, Nue. The violence had the crime rate sky-high in the Elm City since the kidnapping of Ms. Edwards. New Haven homicide detectives were looking for Demi G for questioning for the murders of Lunatic, Ty-Ty and Evelyn.

S.I.U (Special Investigation Unit) had reliable intel that all three murders were connected in relation to the kidnapping of Ms. Edwards. The New Haven Homicide Unit is working with the United States Government. They're focusing their investigation on the notorious Hill Brother's only crew and their drug operation. Truly, there isn't any real concrete evidence on Demi

G to charge him for any of the crimes. So, detectives have been looking for him for about 8 months now, in the hope maybe, just maybe, he would break.

- - -

- Bangor, Maine -

Demi G just walked outside on the porch of the house he just purchased under his girl's name, on Blue Hill East. Demi G fired up his blunt, taking a long pull and deeply inhaled it.

"Boo Boo, isn't it just beautiful out here to be close to summertime?" Nue said.

"Yes, it is, just too damn chilly. But bae, we got to deal with it right now until shit cools down back home." Said Demi G.

"Boo Boo are you kidding me? You already know shit is never going to cool down in New Haven. Sade said the town is hot as fish grease!" Said Nue.

Sade been giving Nue the 411 on what has been going on in the Elm City ever since Demi G went missing in action.

Sade was upset with Ghost about keeping her in the dark, about having Dawg and Black murdered. She still had no knowledge on why Ghost had them both smoked, which had Sade mad as fuck with Joey Ghost shit. Sade is Nue's oldest cousin and they always been close.

"As long as she continues fucking Greatness we cool, but I also need her to get back right with Ghost." Said Demi.

Demi G was pissed that Joey Ghost, Greatness and Mary were still alive, even though he wanted to be the one to put a bullet in their heads personally. He still wouldn't mind if someone would've knocked them off before he could get a chance, because the law has been on his heels.

Nue came walking to the porch from the living room, and hugged Demi G from the back.

"Boo Boo, I love you so much." Nue said, before kissing Demi G on the cheek.

"I love you more, baby!"

Chapter Twenty - Eight

2005

Another year passed, it's 2005. The Elm City cooled down in the streets as with the beef. Niggas was back to getting money again. Demi G owed Chuyloco $500,000 and didn't see Chuy since he left town. He sent word to Loco that he was on the run and the authorities were on his line. Demi G knew that after all this time, he couldn't see Chuyloco without having his $500,000. Demi G only had $250,000 to his name. He left about $500,000 in the streets before he left, and there was too much beef going on. So, he couldn't fault some of his niggas for fucking up some of his bread. Beef is expensive!

Demi G was finally back in the Elm. Of course, he was still low-key playing behind 15% tints. He was trying to figure out how to get his money back and murder Joey Ghost, Greatness and Mary. Nue rented out the new 2005 Dodge Charger from Hertz. You could hear the hemi super-charged engine roar as Demi G drove up church St. downtown. Demi G was cruising when he noticed the Ghetto Boys about four cars back behind him, following.

"Baby, that's Messy and Larry Love's four cars behind us in that black four door Honda Accord?" Asked Demi G.

"Yes! Boo Boo that's them G niggas!" Nue said, as she pulled out her Glock 9.

"Ayo cuz... I'm trying to get closer to these fucking Mexicans." Said Messy.

The Mexican cartel was the next car behind Demi. Messy and Larry Love had no idea that Demi G was in front of the Mexican being pursued.

"Cuz, we in the middle of downtown! Messy, this shit is hot as fuck!" Said Larry Love.

"Joey Ghost said it's on sight! So, you know what the fuck on sight means." Said Messy.

Chuyloco had a contract on Demi G's head. His cartel was ordered to kill him wherever they saw him at. Nue was ready to bust her Glock.

"Baby, I'ma bust this turn right on Chapel St. once I make the turn, start firing on them G niggas!" Demi G told Nue.

The light turned green and Nue hung out the passenger side window .... Mocka, Mocka, Mocka, Mocka, Mocka, Mocka,! Nue was letting off at the G niggas' car.

"Oh, shit amigo! One of the Mexican said as he started firing back at the charger."

Larry Love put his tek-9 out of the window and let it rip at the cartel..........

Tat, tat, tat, tat, tat, tat, tat, tat, tat, tat, tat.

Mocka, Mocka, Mocka, Mocka, Mocka, Mocka……..

Demi G put the Dodge Hemi to work speeding up Chapel St. disappearing into traffic.

Larry Love was spraying every bullet he could into the car of the Mexicans until the Mexican crashed right into a parked car.

"They had someone behind us following us the entire time. Shit! I'm hit…..in my arm!" Said by one of the cartel members.

"I'm hit too! In my left shoulder! They killed Jose! Come on before the cops get here!" One of the Mexicans said. before they fled the scene.

"Boo Boo, someone else was shooting at us! They looked like Spanish, babe." Said Nue.

"You said Spanish?" Asked Demi G.

"Yes, they were." Said Nue.

"Damn. They had to be the cartel." Said Demi G.

Demi G immediately grabbed his phone to call Chuyloco but the number was disconnected.

"Fuck….Damn! Baby, his shit been disconnected!" Said Demi G.

"Boo Boo, Everything's going to be okay!" Nue said, trying to calm her man's ass down.

200

"Once I saw one of the Mexicans with a gun in their hand, I started shooting at them too!" Said Nue.

"I wonder if you hit any of them...Cartel or G niggas!"

- - -

- Demi G -

Demi G was on the run from the law, Black Flags, Gee niggas, and the Cartel.

Demi G and Nue was staying at the crib of Nue's aunty on Cedar Hill Ave. Cedar Hill was the last place anyone would expect Demi G would be laying low. Cedar Hill neighborhood is a very quiet part of New Haven, and majority of the people that live there are seniors and college students that attend Yale University. Demi G decided to walk to the Hess gas station on State St. around the corner.

Mentally, Demi G was exhausted. He's been dealing with a lot of stress lately. Demi G knew that since he had multiple enemies, he had to be extra-on-point from them and the law, if it came to that.

Demi G crossed the street on his way to buy some Dutchess. It was lightly raining, so there was only a few people walking up and down the busy State St. As soon Demi G finished buying his Dutchess, this white man pulled into the gas station in an all-white four-door Audi A8. When he stepped out of his car, Demi G put his hoodie over his head when he wanted to pass the strange white-guy.

"Hey Demi Edwards" The white guy yelled in Demi G's direction. Demi G looked back. knowing that no one ever called him by his government name. Demi reached for his Glock.

"Hey, hey, hey... There's no need for all that!" Said the white guy.

The white guy threw his hands up in a joking manner and said, "Relax Demi G, there's really no need for any of that! I'm from the dream team, I'm here to help you."

"The dream team? What the fuck is the dream team?" Said Demi G, confused.

"Ain't that some Olympic shit with Michael Jordan, Magic and them." Said Demi G.

The white guy just started laughing.

"Yeah, that's right, and who was the dream team playing for?" Asked the white guy.

"The United States of America." Said Demi G.

"Ding, ding, ding! You're absolutely correct Mr. Edwards. Well, I also play for the United States of America. I'm part of the dream team. A.K.A. the F.B.I.," said the white guy.

As soon as Demi G heard the white man say F.B.I., he released his grip off his Glock. This was every street nigga worst fear...... Federal government.

"So, what do you want with me." Asked Demi G.

"I'm Agent Davis, Mathew Davis to be precise. But you can just call me Matt." said Agent Davis introducing himself.

"Look kid, I know you got a gun on you and I understand that at this point in time you need it. I'm not here to charge you for no gun. Look Demi G, the F.B.I. and I are offering you help. Help us and we'll help you, we need you to come downtown to Orange St. to start up the process for a proffer between you and the dream team." Said Agent Davis.

"What....? For what?" Asked Demi G.

"Look Demi G, we're investigating the city's biggest racketeering indictment that New Haven has ever seen and you play a heavy role in our investigation. So, Mr. Edwards, help us help you!" Said Agent Davis.

"I'm not helping anyone! And I'm not going anywhere near Orange St!" Said Demi G.

Demi G started to walk away and stopped once he heard the agent say, *"you are part of the notorious Elm City Brothers (E.C.B.) Y'all are at war with the Mexican cartel. The war started in the 89's, the Elm City brothers were founded in*

Cheshire Correctional Institution, All the neighborhood came together in New Haven and forms E.C.B. to protect each other from rival gangs. In 1988, most of them came home, deciding to keep the unity that was built in prison. E.C.B. got involved in the city's drug trade and started to contribute to the rise of New Haven's crime rate. Joey Ghost has always been the leader of the Elm City brothers."

"They went to war with Chuyloco and his Mexican cartel members over the drug trade in the Elm City. This war actually has been going since the late 80's. Throughout the 90's, Chuyloco been recruiting guys from the Elm City Brothers to be a part of his cartel. This is the main reason why majority of the neighborhood been at war with each other. So when a young thorough breed like yourself jump off the porch into the game, you really can't answer the question on why you are even beefing with rival neighborhoods in the first place. A few years back, Dark-Skin Jack got murdered. He was also an original member of the E.C.B., and we know that Joey Ghost was the one who sent that hit in order to get him out of the way to control the Hill. Dark-Skin Jack was getting his product from Black and Dawg. Both of them had ties to Chuyloco's cartel, and were also murdered by a hit from Ghost."

"Joey Ghost is the President of the Elm City Brothers and each neighborhood has a captain in the drug game. Elm City Brothers pledged an oath that each member took while

serving their time. Joey Ghost was the enforcer of the oath that Mr. Edwards, which is you, and your H.B.O. crew are nothing compared to this empire. We were investigating Dark-Skin Jack and Dee Gotti. Somehow, Dee Gotti got wind of our investigation and next thing you know our informant, Lunatic got killed. Murdered by an order given by you! For the kidnapping of your mother. See, I know you're not a murderer, Mr. Edwards, and you killing Lunatic while Joey Ghost have your mother in custody don't make any sense. Then there's Evelyn, who we believe was murdered by H.B.O for setting up Ty-Ty for Joey Ghost!"

Demi G just stood there, stuck lost for words. He has been hearing of the Elm City Brothers, but never had knowledge that Joey Ghost was the leader of E.C.B.

Demi G was always told as a youngin that the game was much bigger than Demi G could imagine. Demi G was now realizing that he was just a pawn in Chuyloco's plan to sell his product in the Elm and take over the entire city. Demi G felt used.

Demi G thought back to that night back in 1997, when we went on that mission with the Ghetto Boys to murder those Mexicans. Then there was that big trash-bag that Sade had come out of the house with. That trash-bag had to be filled with kilos of cocaine... which made that a whole set-up for a robbery.

A thousand and one questions were running through Demi G's head...Lunatic was an informant? And who smoked him? Did the Candy Girls set up Ty-Ty? And who did Joey Ghost pay for the hit?

Oooh Shit. It's all starting to make sense a little. Demi G thought to himself.

The other day, them Gee niggas were trying to kill them Mexicans. Not us? But the Mexicans were trying to kill us though...... Joey Ghost had Dark-Skin Jack murdered. How is that?

Oooh Shit, I did take over the Hill after that, but I was working for Joey Ghost......Damn, Ty-Ty was my guy, why did Joey Ghost have him killed? Rickita is his daughter, so she had to have helped him line it up.

We didn't kill Evelyn, or did we? Who killed her without letting me know? Joey Ghost is rich! Why would he ask for $500,000 for the ransom of my mom? ......Ty-Ty, Lunatic, and Lee died the same day and my mother kidnapped that same exact night! I don't know what to believe anymore! Demi G said to himself.

"Look, Agent Davis. I'm not going anywhere to talk to no one's dream team so that's out!" said Demi G. "We will be back to talk to you, but the next time, you will be indicted! I gave you an offer to join the dream team." Said Agent Davis.

"Look cuz, it's out!" Said Demi G, as he started back walking down Cedar Hill Ave.

Demi G knows the Feds were the best of liars, but he still was a little scared because the Feds knew too much and too many details that made it obvious that someone was telling them everything. Demi got back in the house... *"Baby, pack our shit! We're getting the fuck out of here."* Said Demi G.

"Why? What are you talking about?" Asked Nue.

"Cause we're under investigation by the dream team!"

"What's the dream team?" Asked Nue.

"The F.B.I.!!!!"

Chapter Twenty - Nine

2006

Niantic Correctional Institution for Females.

It was June 16, 2006, all the women that were incarcerated there were in celebration after hearing about the release of some that were the most hated. She was the bully of all the bullies there at the prison. She was being released early due to her victory in winning her 2254 motion on lack of evidence. She had her conviction lifted. The females weren't happy or celebrating her victory in court, they were celebrating the fact that they would no longer have to be bullied and oppressed.

As she got in front of the prison, she finally was able to have a smell of freedom. The air was clear, it was nice outside, and the sky was clear blue.

"Killa Can!" Rickita had yelled from her pink 2006 Benz G Wagon.

"Hey lil cuz! Damn Kita, I missed you so much." Said Killa.

Killa had got thick ass as hell! Her ass was always big, but with all the weight she gained, she was thicker than a snicker. Fat-asses ran in her family's bloodline. She had her natural hair braided back in long cornrows down to her ass.

"Big cousin, I missed you so much! Get in the truck, bitch.... I'm taking you shopping and getting you out of those clothes A.S.A.P." Said Kita.

"Yeah, I know..... But first, call your father, I just did a long time. Me and that bitch-ass nigga got some unfinished business to handle. That motherfucker tried to have me murdered and fucked around, and got two of his hitters killed." Said Killa.

"Listen cuz, fuck all that right now! You need to get you some dick in you!" Said Kita.

"Bitch, I'm gay as fuck. I done fall in love with some pussy!"

"O.M.G.!" Said Kita.

"Now, like I said, we have some unfinished business.....Text Chuyloco, and let him know the original Candy Girl is home!!!"

- - -

- 1996 -

Nashawn and Demi hopped on the City bus on Congress Ave, on their way to play ball at the open gym at Webster. Every neighborhood in New Haven had an open gym or some kind of after-school program for the youth, to help them stay out of trouble. Webster is a school in the Tribe neighborhood. Nashawn always wanted to display his sick-basketball talent and

Webster's open gym was the talk of the town. All the best players wanted to play ball there, but what Nashawn and Demi G didn't understand was why only certain hoods were allowed to play.

"Ayo cuz, you always want to go and show off. Got us going all the way to the Tribe, I hate going to other projects since the last time I got jumped in the G, but I get it tho...I'm with you." Said Demi G.

"Shit, it's fun as hell dunking on these niggas, plus I heard there are mad chicks there. Your little girlfriend crush is going to be there anyway.... Little pretty Nue.... Ha, ha, ha." Nashawn said, while laughing at his right-hand man.

"Man shut up with that Nue shit." Said Demi.

"Nigga, you ain't got to lie to me! That's the only real reason why you going .... To see Nue!" said Nashawn.

They got off the B-bus and boarded the D-bus going to Dixwell Ave.

"I got something to tell you, Demi." Said Nashawn.

"What you got to tell me?" Demi asked.

"I got down with Stevens Street Posse." Said Nashawn.

All throughout the 80's Stevens street was known for being a million-dollar block and also known for its violence.

"Damn. You really got down with S.S.P.?" Asked Demi.

"Hell yeah! They got all the power, especially Dre, Mone Lush, and Disco. I look up to them niggas."

They approached Webster's on Dixwell Ave, both Nashawn, and Demi G were nervous, walking by the Tribe projects to get to Webster's. They entered the community center; it had about 200 kids all over Webster. There were about 100 in the big gym, and they all was from the Tribe. Demi and Nashawn headed towards the bleachers. Nashawn took his shorts and kicks out of his book-bag and called Next, Demi just looked around, while he sat next to Nashawn until he saw Nue.

Nue walked over to them both from a crowd of Tribe chicks.

"I told you not to come here," Said Nue

" I know, but you never told me why?" Said Demi

"Because Demi, it's Tribe only here." Said Nue.

On the other side of the gym there were two heavyset 12-year-olds, the same age as Nashawn and Demi. Shana walked over to them and asked, *"where y'all from?"*

Demi got his ass whooped in the G a couple years back for this same shit, but in the Elm, if you ain't claiming your hood, you are considered a bitch!

211

"The Hill." Demi and Nashawn said at the same time to Shana. Shana turned around to where Pizzy and Bout It were at, and yelled to them, *"The Hill!!!"*

The whole gym got quiet. *"See, I told you Demi; you shouldn't have come here!"*

Demi and Nashawn just sat there as they watched two big ass-niggas walk towards them.

"Damn! We bout to get our ass whooped! Fucking with you, Nashawn!" said Demi.

"I don't give a fuck! Fuck these Tribe niggas, it's whatever." Said Nashawn.

"Hold the fuck up! Where y'all from?" Asked Pizzy.

"Nigga! I said I'm from the fucking Hi.....CRACCK!"

Pizzy punched Nashawn in the mouth before he could finish saying the word Hill. CRACKKK! Bout It hooked off on Demi. Both of them were trying to make run for it, but there were too many of them everywhere. Demi and Nashawn were swinging-straight haymakers. Demi managed to get free and left through the emergency exit, but realized Nashawn wasn't by his side. So Demi ran back to get his best friend and saw about 20 Tribe-niggas taking turns, punching and kicking his best friend. Demi looked around trying to find a weapon, he saw a fire extinguisher and grabbed it off the wall. Demi ran into the gym and started spraying it on all the faces of them Tribe-niggas.

"Nigga, come on!" Demi yelled to Nashawn. Nashawn's eyes was fucked up bad, he could barely see. Demi grabbed his arm.

"Come on Nashawn." Said Demi, as the Tribe-niggas struggled to see through the cloud of white smoke from the fire extinguisher.

"Run nigga!" Said Demi. They both ran out of the gym. Nue led them to another exit door, so as to go outside before they ran into more Tribe niggas. They were running their fastest through the Tribe.

"Oh shit! We can't even get on the bus. I left my book-bag with all my stuff in it." Said Nashawn.

"Fuck that book-bag! We all fucked up, we might as well walk home." Said Demi. And that's what they did. Once they got to Stevens street in the Hill, they were happy.

"I knew we shouldn't have went there Nigga." Said Demi.

"You wanted to see Nue, so, stop fronting." Said Nashawn.

"Yeah and I got my ass whooped right in front of her." Said Demi.

"Fuck it! We got our ass whooped!" They both started laughing.

"I love you, bro." said Demi.

"I love you too, bro!" Nashawn said.

"We are best friends for life! We ain't never going to let nothing get between us bro!" Said Demi.

"Pinky swears!"

Demi and Nashawn locked pinkes, and both said, *"Best friends forever…. For life."*

"O yeah, another thing." Said Nashawn.

"What?" Asked Demi.

"We going to keep tonight a secret between us!" Said Nashawn. They both started laughing, thinking about how they had to run from getting beaten to death.

"Okay, brothers for life. Our secret." Said Demi.

"Brothers to the end!" Said Nashawn. They embraced one another with a hug.

Chapter Thirty

Present 2006

Demi G got the drop on Greatness and Mary. Tonight, was the night for Demi G to get even once and for all. Demi G was laying low and broke with little to no money to his name. Nue took their last $150,000 and invested in a three-family foreclosed home. They were struggling to obtain tenants. Demi G left the drugs game alone because of his run-in with the FEDS that day at the gas station. But, he still didn't have any intentions of letting them Black Flag niggas and Joey Ghost get away with kidnapping his mom and killing Ty-Ty. Sade kept close ties to Greatness for Demi G. Now, it was time to put Greatness in the ground where he belonged

- - -

- November 12, 2006 at 9:00pm -

Demi G bought a 2004 Honda Accord. All-black and tinted down. He got the drop that Greatness and Mary was staying in a studio apartment on Emerson St. in West ville. Demi G was dressed in all-black, with a goon mask over his face. He parked on fountain St., the street Emerson St. is off of.

Demi G got butterflies in his stomach, nervous about if things didn't go his way, and what would be the result at the end. Demi G knew this was the time to finally get even with Greatness for all the fuck-shit he did to him. He wasn't going to fuck up this opportunity.

Demi G went in through the back. He crept inside the cracked door that Sade left open. Sade was talking to Mary and Greatness in the bedroom. All of this looked and sounded too familiar. Demi G had a firm grip on his glock as he walked down the hallway until he came to the room where the voices were coming from.

"No one fucking move!" Said Demi G.

"Oh shit, please don't shoot!" Said Mary.

"Shut the fuck up stupid bitch!" BLOCKA!

Demi G put one bullet right in the face of Mary while she was laying down on the bed. Sade walked out to the room.

"Oh, you stupid bitch…… This hoe set me up!" Said Greatness. Talking about Sade when she left the room.

"Bitch-nigga why you ain't shoot me?" Said Greatness. Demi G pulled his mask off. He had tears in his eyes.

"Damn cuz, you kidnapped my mom. Killed Ty-Ty, staged the beef with the Tre with smoking Black and Dawg, robbing my spots, and the whole time you fucking my bitch behind my back! Nigga, you ain't my friend! You ain't the best friend that I grew up with!" Said Demi G.

"You soft-ass nigga, this is all about some pussy?" Asked Greatness, while smiling at Demi G.

"Nigga, don't take this out of context! This is about betrayal." Said Demi G.

"Then you go and kill my bitch, Mary, right in front of me?" Said Greatness.

"My mother told me to kill her first and make you watch." Demi G said in a low voice.

The crazy thing was Greatness never showed any fear to anyone, but tonight was a little different. It was personal. Demi G didn't want to really kill his best friend, but he kidnapped his mother and killed Ty-Ty. Greatness was a relentless, ruthless killer that had to be put down. The world definitely would be better place with Greatness gone.

"Demi, you ain't no killer." Said Greatness.

"Shut the fuck up!" Said Demi G, trying to build up the courage to kill his ex-best friend.

"(Lil cuz, you gotta bust your cherry)" is what was playing in his head from back in the days that Joey Ghost told him when he caught his first body. Fuck Joey Ghost is what Demi G told himself.

Blocka, Blocka, Blocka, Blocka!

Demi G shot Greatness all in his chest! He kept telling himself

"I had to.... I had to kill.......... He violated!"

"Nigga....... Don't move!" Said Sade, while she pointed a 357 magnum to the back of Demi's head.

Joey Ghost walked in the room clapping his hands and said, "CHECKMATE!"

About the Author

Don Chramaine Ogman, popularly known as Maine or Maineyo. He was born and raised in New Haven, Ct 06519. He is 40 years old and a father of 4.

Maineyo went through a lot growing up in the cold Elm City, and for the last decade, and has been in the Federal Penitentiary fighting for his freedom. He fell victim to the harsh crack cocaine disparity; 280 grams of crack that got him 188 months with the ten years mandatory minimum.

Nevertheless, his years of being incarcerated has made him become a positive role model, not just for himself, but for his kids and everybody around him.

This is Maineyo's first book and he plans on writing more urban novels in the nearest future. With this work of fiction, Maineyo wants to bring to the urban book readers about his city...Elm city.

www.ingramcontent.com/pod-product-compliance
Lightning Source LLC
Chambersburg PA
CBHW060921250626
47159CB00008B/3111